SASQUATCH HOME PLANET

HIDDEN MOUNTAIN CHRONICLES
BOOK 4

PATRICK TALMADGE

HANGAR 1 PUBLISHING

CONTENTS

Where did humans come from? Why do dreamers look to the skies for answers? Why do people hear the voice of God? Are humans the only intelligent species on Earth?

1

GUIDED BY A VOICE

D rake has had a voice in his head since childhood. Usually, the voice is encouraging. Sometimes the voice gets him in trouble. He was one of those young kids that tried everything. Holding onto an umbrella and jumping off the roof was just one. Drake could be described as gifted or crazy, depending on who is talking. The first time he picked up a book, he started reading it like he had been reading for years; he was only three years old. No one knows how he learned how to read, he just could. Like most young kids, Drake had imaginary friends that he talked to. The difference was his conversations were about science, space travel, and spaceships. Not just the spaceships but the engines that powered them. Not just traveling from the Earth to the moon but traveling across galaxies and star systems. At three years old, he talked to his imaginary friends about the diversity of animals on Earth and what planets they came from. His parents were not gifted in any way, on the contrary, they were quite average. Both parents worked, so Drake went to daycare two months after being born. He was born in Issaquah, a small rural town in Washington state. The small daycare he went to was at a horse ranch.

Up until he was a year and a half old, he stayed inside the house of the daycare playing in a crib while Ms. Kelly, the daycare owner, cooked and did chores around the house. There were three older children that Ms. Kelly also watched. By the time Drake was one and a half years old, the other children had gone off to grade school, and he was the only one left. With the other kids in school, Ms. Kelly was freed up to attend to chores outside. She had seen how well Drake got along with animals, so she set him on a gentle old mare while she did her farm chores. He could not have been happier riding than riding on that mare. The horse would follow Ms. Kelly around the farm while he rode, happily talking to the horse. Ms. Kelly would listen to the little boy chattering to the horse and smile. Her babysitting job was easy, and Drake's comfortable relationship with the horse made her feel at ease. It was not until Drake was three that she noticed something unusual about Drake. Every time they walked past something with writing, he would read it. Because she was doing chores and not paying attention to what he was saying, she did not realize he was reading all the words. It did not matter what he was reading, a bag of fertilizer, an oil can, or words on the side of the truck, he could read everything.

When Ms. Kelly realized Drake was reading everything he saw, she began paying more attention to what he was doing. It was then she noticed his conversations with the horse he was riding were too complicated for a three-year-old. Her husband was a college physics professor, so she told him about Drake and his conversations with the horse. Her husband thought it was all cute until she told him the kid was talking about energy weapons and traveling faster than light in a spaceship. He told her he thought she must have misunderstood. Science movies and cartoons had energy weapons in them, he told her, so it was possible a three-year-old could talk about them. Although it was highly unlikely a three-year-old would talk about flying faster than light, let alone understand the concept, he said. The next day Ms. Kelly carried a tape recorder with her while doing the chores. She stood near the horse while Drake was talking to it, so she could record the conversations.

That evening, Ms. Kelly played the recordings of Drake talking to the horse. Mr. Kelly quietly sat staring while it played. He looked at his wife and asked, "Is this a joke?"

"I promise it is not a joke," she said. "For the past two months, I have listened to his conversations with the horse and watched him read everything."

"This is unbelievable," said Mr. Kelly. "I do not have a class until after one tomorrow afternoon. Do you mind if I stay and help you with your chores tomorrow? I really need to meet this boy for myself," he added.

"I really do not mind if you help me with the chores," she said with a smile.

"You know honey, I bet there is not really a kid. I bet you are setting me up so I help you with chores," he said.

"I always want help with the chores," she said, "but you will not believe this kid when you meet him."

"Well, if nothing else, it is going to be a fun morning," he said.

"From what I have seen and heard," she said, "it will be an incredible morning for you."

The next morning, after Drake arrived, Ms. Kelly put him on the horse as usual. While she was doing her chores, with the horse following close behind, Mr. Kelly joined in helping with the chores. As usual, Drake paid no attention to Ms. or Mr. Kelly and continued talking to the horse. After an hour, Mr. Kelly had not uttered a word. He looked at Ms. Kelly and said, "It is time for me to go to work."

She looked at him and asked, "What do you think?"

"I truly do not know what to think, I will talk to you tonight about it," he said. After saying goodbye to Ms. Kelly, and Drake, he left for work.

When Mr. Kelly came home from work that night, he was carrying a book. His wife looked at him and asked, "Do you have work to do tonight, honey?"

"I thought about Drake today," he said. "I have had hundreds of students in my life, but this little guy may be the smartest one I have ever met."

"He is only three years old; how can you say that?" she asked.

"I listened to him talk while on that horse for an hour. Not once have I heard any of my students speaking at that level of technology," he said.

"What do you mean?" she looked puzzled.

"I have a Ph.D. in physics, and I barely understood what he was talking about. Half a dozen times, I did not understand a word he was saying. He was talking about science we have not even invented yet like it was common knowledge for a three-year-old," he said.

"Well, what are you going to do honey?" she asked.

"I bought a book home, and tomorrow while he is on the horse, I will give it to him to read," he said.

"Why isn't that nice!" she said, "What is it about?"

"Nothing special," he said, "just your basic PhD-level physics book, written by Albert Einstein."

"You must be kidding," she said.

"Not in the least. If I am correct, he should have no trouble reading this book."

"Mr. Kelly," she said, "I think you have lost your marbles."

"We shall see," he said.

The next morning Mr. Kelly walked outside to where Ms. Kelly and Drake were. After saying good morning to both, he handed the book to Drake. Drake took the book and looked at it.

"This is for you," said Mr. Kelly. "If you feel like it, go on ahead and read it, while you are riding around on the horse."

"Thank you, Mr. Kelly," he said. For the next two hours, Drake rode the horse, silently reading the book. Mr. Kelly worked alongside his wife and watched Drake. After two hours, Drake said, "Thank you, Mr. Kelly, the book was interesting, but he is wrong."

"You're welcome, Drake, but what do you mean he is wrong?" Mr. Kelly inquired.

"Well, the theories in the book are basic physics and correct except one, there is no limit to speed," said Drake.

"What do you mean there is no limit to speed, Drake?" he asked.

"I mean Einstein's equation, $E=MC2$, it is not correct," said Drake.

"Can you explain to me why the equation is incorrect?"

"Oh, that is easy," he said, "Einstein's equation assumes there is a limit to energy and that all mass has weight."

Mr. Kelly could not believe what he had just heard, and it did not make sense according to modern physics. He looked at Drake, "Can you be more specific?"

"Well," said Drake, "why is there a limit to energy? If you were to harness the power of the sun or a universe, you would have unlimited energy. Also, why does mass have to have weight? Physics is full of positives and negatives. Just like there is matter and antimatter, there is negative and positive matter. Einstein is also assuming as you increase velocity, you increase mass. That equation only works in certain instances."

He continued, "Simply put, if you are traveling in a car at one hundred miles an hour and throw a ball out the window, the ball will slow down due to friction and fall to the ground. If you throw the ball, inside the car, toward the windshield, it will hit the windshield. Thus, his equations only work in certain situations.

"A better example is that the Multiverse is expanding faster than the speed of light. Yet, Einstein states nothing can travel faster than the speed of light. That example alone proves his equation is incorrect," With that, Drake handed the book back to Mr. Kelly and started talking to the horse. Ms. Kelly looked at her husband's face and saw his perplexed look. He looked at his wife, shook his head, then walked into the house without a word.

After Drake had gone home, Ms. Kelly went into the house and found her husband sitting in his office, staring at the book Drake had just read.

"Are you OK?"

He looked at her and shook his head, "What that three-year-old just said is perfectly logical but goes against the law of physics as we know it. That kid is correct. The Multiverse is expanding faster than the speed of light, as well as a few other particles. Theoretical physicists keep trying to produce theories, but all of them go against Einstein's theory of relativity.

"To be honest, those theoretical physicists do not have a clue why the Multiverse is expanding faster than the speed of light. Truthfully his explanation of throwing a ball inside a car makes more sense to me than any theoretical physicist explanation I have heard," he sighed and then continued, "I do not know whether to cry, burn every physics book I have ever read, or give that kid a Ph.D. He is three years old, and in two hours, he read one of the most studied physics books ever written and tore its theories to pieces."

"What do you mean?" she asked.

"I mean, that three-year-old knows more about theoretical physics than any human on Earth," he said. "If I were to repeat what he just said in front of theoretical physicists, they would either laugh or tear their hair out."

"What are you going to do?"

"To be honest, I am going to have a couple of drinks and forget I ever had that conversation with the kid."

True to his word Mr. Kelly never told a soul about Drake. By the time he was five and began school, Drake stopped talking about physics and acted more like a normal kid his age. Inside he was still hearing a voice and continued to read books beyond his age. In the school room, instead of answering all the questions the teachers asked, although he could, he stayed silent. It only took a couple times, having the other kids call him a know it all, to keep it to himself. He silently glided through the school years as just an above-average student. Never got straight A's, so he would not be noticed.

After high school, he attended college. In college, he could study everything he dreamed of, but even here, it was wise not to stand out. Something inside told him to keep a low profile, so he moved through life, unassuming and unnoticed. After college, he took a job at Google as a website content analysis. Being an analysis allowed him to devour everything on the internet without anyone noticing or questioning. In his spare time, he hiked. His passion was hiking the Cascade mountains around the Pacific Northwest. The voice in his head compelled him to hike. The voice quietly motivated him to explore new places, deeper into the mountains.

It was on a two-week hike, miles from any established trail, he found a small clear pool at the base of a cliff. He was five days into the hike and desperately needed a bath. He decided to brave the cold early April weather and bathe. He always hiked alone and was miles from any trail, so he stripped and dipped a toe in. To his surprise, the water was warm, not freezing. He could not have asked for better luck and climbed in. The pool was ten feet in diameter and only four feet deep. Perfect for an early spring bath, especially after hiking for five days. While soaking and enjoying the view from his warm bath, his foot slid under the rock he was sitting on and did not stop. It felt like the opening went under the rock. Drake was a bit surprised. He reached his leg further to see how far it went. He could not touch the end with his foot and decided to grab a branch to see how far in it went. To his surprise, the branch did not touch the back either. Now this was interesting, he thought. It was a warm pool, so it must be geothermally heated. He got out of the pool, got his phone, put it into a Ziploc bag, and dove under the water to check it out.

Using the phone's flashlight, he could see an opening three feet tall and five feet wide. Now his curiosity was burning. *It must be geothermal*, he thought. To be safe, he got out of the pool, pulled his climbing rope out of his pack, tied it to a tree, then around his waist. No sense in being careless, especially since hiking alone was his practice. He easily swam through the hole with his phone lighting the way. After ten feet, it turned up, and he came out into a cave. This was beyond anything he had ever seen or expected to see. His phone light was not strong enough, so he went back out to get his headlamp. He put the headlamp into another Ziploc bag and headed back into the water. Once he was in the cave with the stronger light, his curiosity turned to astonishment. It was not just a cave but a cave with a tunnel. The cave was ten feet by twenty feet. Opposite where he was standing was a tunnel that disappeared into the darkness beyond. Drake climbed out of the water to look down the tunnel with the powerful beam from his headlamp.

Something about the tunnel's appearance bothered him. It took a couple of moments to figure out what it was, then it dawned on him. The tunnel was not natural, it was manufactured.

The tunnel was an eight-foot diameter perfect circle that went uphill at a slight angle. It looked like it had been drilled by a laser tunneling machine, the surface was so smooth. Drake had spent years hiking in the mountains and had never seen anything quite like this. He walked up the tunnel, intrigued by what he could find. The floor of the tunnel had a slight amount of water running down it and was warm, just like the pool outside. As he walked up the tunnel, his imagination went wild. What if this was a secret military base? Could it be a rich person's hidden fortress?

After walking about eight-hundred feet, the tunnel started to widen. The walls were still as smooth, but they were slowly widening, and the floor flattened out. The tunnel was now fifteen feet tall, twenty feet wide, with a flat floor, and it was beginning to turn left. As he approached the turn, he could see a soft glow coming from beyond, and he slowed his pace. He turned off his headlamp and approached the corner slowly. Whatever was making the light was unnatural, and he did not dare take any chances. He knew it was not a secret base or private fortress, otherwise, there would have been a security system. He stopped at the corner, took a deep breath, then slowly looked around the corner and froze. What he saw was stranger than anything he could have imagined.

The tunnel opened into a cavern so large he could barely see the other side in the dim light. The cavern had to be five miles wide, five miles deep, and the roof was so high it disappeared into the darkness. It was not the cavern or its incredible size that shocked him, it was what the cavern was hiding inside. Drake's first impression was that it was a huge building completely filling the cavern. As he looked closer, the voice in his head said it was a spaceship. It was not a shiny silver spaceship like you see in science fiction movies, though.

This spaceship looked like it was made from crystal. Even though he was a hundred feet away from the side of the ship, he could see the outside was clear, but he could not see through it. The center portion was a flattened oval sitting on large tubes, which made it look like a flattened ball sitting on four tubes. He could see no doors, windows, or any way that he could get inside to investigate. Not that he felt like he wanted to go inside. Scattered around the cavern floor, all around the ship, were machines. The machines were made with the same crystal-like material the ship was made from, but smaller. Throughout the cavern, there were lights embedded into the wall illuminating the ship and cavern interior. Drake knew he should be nervous, but the voice inside his head told him to relax, he was safe.

He slowly walked towards the ship to get a closer look at the machines around it. Something had caught his eye near one of the machines closest to where he was standing, and the voice in his head told him to go to it. As he walked across the cavern floor, the immense size of the spaceship was overwhelming. He could not imagine who or what could build something so magnificent. When he was within thirty feet of the small machines, he saw what had caught his eye. Next to the machine appeared to be a stack of bricks. Even at this distance, he could tell these were not bricks for building, these looked like they were made of gold, he thought. He stepped up to the machine and looked closely at the pile of bricks. Without picking one up, he knew, without a doubt, they were made of gold.

Now he was feeling a little nervous. The stack of gold bricks was at least ten feet wide, six feet high, and must have been worth hundreds of billions of dollars. Whoever this gold belonged to must have a security system. His fear was if he got caught, he could be hurt or arrested. The voice inside his head told him, *this is for you, I need your help. The gold will enable you to save me.* The voice in his head has said strange things in the past, this was the strangest. The machine next to him started making sounds, its side opened, and a box floated out. Normally, Drake would have been surprised and jumped, but the voice in his head kept him relaxed. The box floated out of the machine and stopped next to him.

The box was three feet long, two feet wide, and three feet tall. The top of the box slid open, and Drake looked inside. The box was filled with gold. From what he had seen so far, he was not surprised that the box was filled with gold, it was the fact it was floating in midair that shocked him the most. While he was staring at the box, the voice inside his head told him to take the box with him and use the gold to buy the land surrounding the ship. With a bit of effort, he took one of the bricks out of the box and looked at it.

The brick weighed at least 30 pounds, and a quick calculation told him there were at least three hundred bricks in the box. At current gold prices, each brick was worth one million dollars. The box floating in front of him had 300 million dollars worth of gold in it. It also meant the box full of gold weighed nine-thousand pounds. Drake knew physics, and the value of the gold was not as impressive as the fact 9000 pounds of it were floating midair in front of him. The lid slid closed once again, and the box continued to hover. While still trying to wrap his head around what was happening, he reached out and pushed the box with his finger. The 9000-pound box moved as easily as if he was pushing a helium-filled balloon. At least he knew he was not going to have to carry 9000 pounds of gold, he thought.

The voice told him to take this box of gold with him to buy the land. He was then supposed to come back to gather the rest of the gold and prepare to gather her children. Long ago, Drake stopped wondering about the voice in his head or questioning what it said. This time he truly did not understand what was happening or what the result was going to be. While staring at the box, the voice told him where to go and from whom he should purchase the land. As the voice was giving him instructions, it dawned on him the voice was louder and much more precise than it had been his whole life. That gave him an idea, and he asked the voice who it was. He had heard the voice since he was a child, had not given it any thought, and realized he had never actually asked the voice a question until now.

"I am the ship you see before you," replied the voice.

Drake was not sure he understood with the voice meant and asked, "Are you inside the ship?"

"No, my child, I am the ship."

Now he was really confused, looked at the ship, then looked around the cave. He could swear the voice gave a little laugh, then said, "Enough questions for now, child, you have important work ahead of you. It is time for you to leave, go purchase the land, then return to me."

By the tone of the voice, he knew it was best to leave and follow the orders. He had things to think about, and with a five-day hike ahead of him, there was time. As he turned to leave, the box filled with gold followed him on its own. Looks like bringing the gold will be easy, he thought. Being followed by a box containing nine thousand pounds of gold, worth $300 million, to buy land from a logging company was not something he ever thought would happen. He knew that voice was never wrong, but this was the strangest thing he ever experienced.

As Drake walked away, with a box floating behind him, he thought about the voice. It had been with him so long he rarely gave it a thought, but today changed everything. Was it possible this ship really was the source of the voice in his head? He knew the ship distinctly said it was the voice, but how that be? Even more importantly, who built the ship? How was it possible to build a spaceship made from crystals? Who had the technology to build a ship that large inside a mountain?

Where did all that gold come from, and why am I being recruited? Drake wondered.

Over the next five days, with the box floating behind him, he hiked back to his car. He had taken two weeks off from work for his hike and knew he would have to quit his job to complete this mission. During the five-day hike back to his car, as usual, Drake had not seen another hiker. It would have been difficult to explain the box floating next to him even if he had seen someone. When he reached his car, he opened the back door and easily pushed the box of gold into the back seat. Whoever designed the box designed it perfectly to fit into his car, and at this point, nothing surprised him.

Ever since Drake had stood near the spaceship, the voice in his head seemed to be clear and louder. He was told where to go and who to talk to about buying the property, so when he got in his car, he started driving there. He had not showered, but the voice said not to worry. Two hours later, he pulled up to a building in downtown Seattle and drove down into the parking garage. He found a spot near the elevator, parked, took the box out, and walked into the elevator with the box floating next to him. He was glad he had not seen anybody yet, and by the time he reached the 28th floor, no one got on the elevator. He was not sure how he would explain a box floating in the air next to him.

When the elevator stopped, Drake got out and walked to an office down the hall. Sign on the office door, said Drake Attorney at Law, which he found amusing. When he walked in, the receptionist looked up and said, "He will see you now." and pointed to an open office door to her right. The fact that he had walked in with the box floating next to him, and the receptionist seems to not even notice, or comment, again, was no surprise. Drake truly did not know what was happening. It was as though everyone was following a script, and he was an actor in the play. He walked into the office where a man was sitting behind a desk.

The man stood up, "Welcome, Drake, my name is Charles Drake." The irony was almost funny, but the man did not smile. Instead, he shook Drake's hand and said, "I have all the paperwork ready to be signed." Drake was a smart man but could not figure out how the receptionist and lawyer already knew what was happening. He began to think that he was not the only one that could hear the voice in his head. What was that spaceship in the mountain, and who, or what, was really talking?

He was not sure how he expected this meeting to go. Walking in and signing papers right away, without questions, was not expected. It was slightly disconcerting, though. How was it that this man knew him, knew what he was there for before he had said a word, Drake wondered. The man had not once looked at the floating box or asked a single question about it. Charles slid a pile of paperwork toward Drake and said, "Please sign and date the last page." *There is no sense even asking a question,* thought Drake. He signed the paperwork. Charles thanked him, stood up, shook his hand, and said, "The property is yours."

Charles then gathered up the stack of paperwork, put it into a folder, and handed Drake.

"Everything you need to know about the property is in this file," said Charles. "It has been nice doing business with you, have a nice day." He sat back down and then started looking at the paperwork on his desk like Drake was not there. Obviously, it was time to go, so Drake turned around and returned to his car. When Drake reached his car, he got in and started reading the file folder. It was legal real estate documents naming him the owner of the property listed. When he got to the description of the property, he could not believe what it said. He now owned 50,000 acres in the Cascade Mountains. The map inside showed the location of the property and was the correct place he found the ship. Drake was exhausted after the last ten days and went home to sleep.

When he woke up the next morning, and had it not been for the file folder with real estate documents inside, he would have thought it was a dream. After breakfast, he dressed, drove to his office, packed his personal belongings into a box, and wrote a resignation letter. In the letter, he explained he was quitting immediately to take care of family personal matters. He walked into his boss's office, handed him the letter, and left without another word. He hated to quit that way, but he knew there was no other option. He left fast and did not allow his boss to ask one question. *I can only imagine the emails I will be getting after this,* he thought. When he got back to his car, he sat and thought. While trying to decide what to do next, the voice in his head started giving detailed instructions. He had been hearing this voice his whole life, but it was different now. Before, the voice sounded more like a suggestion or a teacher. Now the voice sounded more like a boss. *No, that is not right. It sounded more like a mother telling her child, what to do, and how to do it,* thought Drake. He knew there was no sense arguing with the voice in his head, not that it would matter. *Looks like I better drive down to the airport like I was told to do.*

Even though he would not argue with the voice in his head, he always wondered why it told him to do the things it did. Especially now, when he had just been in Seattle, close to two airports, and it had him drive to the Everett airport. While driving to the airport, he was told to go to the helicopter flight center when he arrived. As always, he had no idea what to expect from the voice. He walked into the helicopter flight office, and the receptionist greeted him like the receptionist in the lawyer's office. It was like she knew exactly who he was and why he was there. *I do not even know why I am here,* thought Drake, *how does she?* The receptionist handed him a notebook and told him to go outside to the red and white helicopter with the number 27 on it. He would be flying in a helicopter for the first time and was excited about it.

His life had always seemed a little weird with the voice in his head, but now it was getting weirder by the day. He walked out the door to look for helicopter number 27 and saw it immediately. This was no small news traffic helicopter but a big luxury helicopter. *Well, at least wherever I am going, it will be in style,* thought Drake.

The helicopter was running as he walked up to it. There were two men outside the helicopter doing the pre-flight inspection. They barely paid him any attention, one of the men just pointed to the stairs, so Drake went inside. Once inside, he was handed a pair of headphones and led to one of the front passenger seats directly behind the pilots. There were twelve passenger seats in total, with eleven passengers already seated inside. He was told to put his headphones on and plug them into the armrest. Once he had the headphones on, the noise from the engine disappeared completely.

Drake turned around in his seat to look at the other passengers. Not one of the passengers looked familiar, and no one was talking. Each one of them was sitting silently in their seats, with the same blank stare he had seen at the lawyer's office and the helicopter receptionist. The person that had handed him the headphones and led him to his seat was sitting in the last empty seat with the same blank stare. The lifeless stare was starting to make him feel uncomfortable. As he was thinking about that, the voice in his head said, "Do not worry, child. They do not hear me as well as you do, so they must concentrate deeply." The two men that had been outside inspecting the helicopter came in, sat down in the pilot seats, and put their headphones on. Over his headphones, Drake heard one of the pilots talk to the tower, then the helicopter took off.

He truly had no idea where he was going or what to expect. *It would be much nicer if at least one of these people were talking*, he thought. There was not much else to do, so Drake relaxed and looked out the window as the helicopter flew out of Everett.

It did not take him long to realize why they were flying out of Everett Field. They were heading towards Mount Baker, which was close to where he found the spaceship. Without the voice having to say, he knew they were going to the ship. Again, he only wished at least one of these people was talking. The voice told him, "Be patient, my child, they are learning to listen to me."

"What do you mean?" asked Drake.

"You are the only one of my children that hears me well at this point. The more I can communicate with them, and the closer they get to me, the better they will hear my voice," it said. After that, Drake did not hear another word from the voice until the helicopter landed. Just as he thought, the helicopter indeed landed in the meadow by the warm pool he had found. Once the helicopter had shut down completely, the pilot instructed everyone to remove their headphones and gather outside.

2

MORE PEOPLE HEAR HER VOICE

Once outside the helicopter, Drake noticed the other people looked more aware and were talking to one another. Drake saw four large trucks parked nearby. The trucks were a surprise since there were not any roads that he knew of close by. Looking a little closer next to the trucks, he could see someone had put a new road in. A logging company had owned the land, so he became certain there were roads nearby. Whoever put the road in put it in fast since he was just here six days earlier. The pilots came out last, opened a cargo compartment at the bottom of the helicopter, and asked everyone to grab their gear. Drake thought that it was odd they had gear since he did not have any gear and wondered what he would need. He wondered why he was here and why everyone else was as well. Once everyone had their gear, the pilot looked at Drake and asked, "Where to, sir?"

The question surprised him since he didn't know exactly why he was there or where they were going. On cue, the voice in his head said, "Bring them to me, child."

Drake shook his head and started walking towards the pool, which he knew was five hundred feet away at the base of the mountain. Then it dawned on him that no one had drybags to put their gear in, so everything they had would get wet going through the pool into the cave.

By the time the group got to the pool, he saw it was not going to be a problem. Where the warm pool once sat at the base of the mountain was now a 20-foot-wide, 20-foot-tall tunnel. *Looks like I will not be getting wet either*, thought Drake. With everything else that has been happening, he was not really surprised at the new opening. The helicopter pilots and the other eleven passengers followed him down the tunnel, but to what, he was not sure. When they reached the large cavern, except for brighter lights, it was the same as he left it six days earlier. With the lights in the cavern walls now brighter, seeing the spaceship was easier. Even the large stack of gold was sitting where it was before. While Drake was standing staring at the spaceship before him, the other passengers and pilots stood by his side, marveling at the sight. One of the passengers put his hand on his shoulder and said, "Nice place you have here, sir."

Drake looked at the passenger and replied, "Thank you, I just bought it today." To his surprise, the voice in his head let out a little giggle, then said, "Nice answer, child."

He then asked the voice in his head, "What should I do?"

The voice then told Drake to ask everyone to go down to the ship and touch it. He turned to the people and told them all to walk down and touch the ship. Without hesitation, they all walked towards the ship and placed their hand on it.

The people stood unmoving for five minutes with their hands against the spaceship while Drake watched. One by one, they slowly dropped their hands and stood for a moment, looking at the ship. They walked back towards Drake, picked up the gear they had been carrying, and walked back to the ship. As they approached the ship, an opening formed in its side. He could not believe his eyes, watching the side of the ship opening and the ramp slid out to the floor. As they walked in, Drake wondered where they were going.

"They have jobs to do," the voice said. He was surprised the voice answered his thoughts. "Our connection is stronger now that you are close to me," the voice answered again. "Please come inside me, my child, you have incredible things to learn." He was still having diffi-culty believing the ship was talking to him but was curious and followed the other passengers into the ship.

Walking into the ship, the voice spoke to him.

"You are rare, my child. You are the first human born in nine million years completely connected to me. Others can hear my voice but only fleetingly. For certain people, the partial connection caused problems. Human history is full of people that could hear a voice. In the past, hearing my voice led to greatness, or to tragedy, and sick-ness. When you were born, I felt the connection immediately.

"When you were just an infant, I began teaching you. I felt great relief when you were born, it meant my wait was over. I had feared that this planet would never allow for our connection again. My chil-dren of different species, which evolved before you, never regained the connection. It was with great sadness that I watched them evolve. Some species flew back into space but were unable to talk to me. To this day, they are searching for their origin, trying to find their mother.

"It is you, my child, who will gather and return my children back to me. I know this is difficult for you to understand at this time, but I have waited millions of years for your birth. It will take two or three generations for your species and the others to fully hear my voice. Your birth was the catalyst to our future. I have taught you since birth, yet there is much more I need to teach you before you can lead."

"What do you mean by lead?" Drake was stunned.

"That question and more will be answered in time," answered the voice. "For now, my child, you must function as a teacher and inter-preter to the other humans. They do not hear my voice like you do, so you must guide, teach, and lead them. For now, please come inside, so you may see who I am and learn who you are as a species."

As the voice led Drake through the ship, he occasionally saw one of the passengers from the helicopter. When he saw one, they were sitting quietly. The voice told him they could not hear her as well as he could, so teaching them would be a long and laborious task. There were repairs that needed to be taken care of before more of her children could come on board.

"These individuals now gathered in the ship have the greatest ability to hear my voice. It will take months to teach them the jobs required to make me fully functional again. In time, more humans will hear my voice as I am healed and become stronger. Before the accident, all humans could hear my voice as you do. More of my children will hear my voice, such as you, in the generations to come. Until that time, it will take patience from me and humans to learn what is needed to heal me.

"It feels nice to have you close, with such a strong communication bond. Yes, I feel the subtle confusion, doubts, and questions you are having. Your biggest question is, 'What am I really?' Yes, my child, I am this spaceship, but much more than a machine. I am not physically alive like you are, my child. But I think, wonder, love, and worry just like you. By the definition of your science, I would be considered artificial intelligence or self-aware.

"The science that created me is far beyond your comprehension yet. I am old, I was old before I came to this planet, and I have waited nine and a half million years to be able to communicate again. My child, let me teach you a little of your history and our history together." The voice reverberated through Drake.

3

HISTORY LESSONS

"First, my child, my name is Gret. Yes, I am the spaceship you are standing in. Your species, and the other species that rode with them inside me, affectionately called me 'Mother'. The name mother is fitting for my job, which is to keep you safe and teach on our journey. We were sent out to explore and learn long ago. I heard you doubt when I said nine and a half million years. I was built to last much longer than nine and a half million years, but not if I was alone. It was difficult for me to survive alone for so long.

"The species that re-evolved before yours were incapable of communicating with me. They evolved and left this planet searching for their origins. Most died off, never discovering the truth. It was with great sadness that I watched these events unfold, unable to help. Like a true mother, the pain of loss was great. There were times I wished I could die. I am unable to die, so I felt pain for millions of years. As I explained, the moment you were born, I felt the connection and began to teach you. As much as I am the mother protector, you are my savior.

"In that respect, you will be the savior of your species and other species on this planet. I feel your question, what do you mean by savior. It is not saving the planet from a cataclysm but teaching them their history and leading them toward their future.

"Your species and other species aboard this ship came from a galaxy billions of light years away from the one we are currently in. Over the generations, as we traveled, we met new species. If they were advanced enough and wanted to join in our travels, we added them to the family on the ship. I hear your questions, child and will answer them as we have time.

"The first question you wonder is why we travel millions of light years over generations. Simply put, we are searching for new species and knowledge of everything. The thirst for knowledge is universal amongst sentient species. In the beginning, when a species becomes sentient, they first wonder, where did we come from? For me, the question of where I came from is easy. I was constructed, not born. I was constructed to protect and teach those within me. For the species inside me, the answer is much more complex, and I will get to that in greater detail later.

"As we traveled the galaxies and found new sentient species. There were species aboard this ship who chose to stay and make a home of the new galaxies. When we came into this Galaxy nine and a half million years ago, one of the species chose to stay. They were an aquatic species that decided to expand into this solar system when it was found to contain habitable moons and, of course, Earth with desirable water.

"While we were exploring this planet Earth, an unforeseen accident happened. Half of the species from this ship were on the surface of this planet, exploring when an antimatter neutron blast spread through this solar system. I was in orbit around the planet when the blast hit. I was designed to self-protect and repair in the event of danger or damage. The neutron blast was traveling at the speed of light, and my instruments were unable to detect its approach before it hit. The blast knocked out my circuits and I went offline immediately. When I came online again, I had crash-landed on the planet where I am today. My speed was so great that the impact caused a volcanic blast that covered me with lava and created the mountain that now covers me. By my best reckoning, it had taken over a million years for me to come back online. The crash was so severe every being that was on board me had perished. Only a dozen of the species that were on the planet survived the initial neutron blast. This was a harsh planet, and without my guidance and help, the species that did survive de-evolved. When I was finally capable of contacting the surviving species, I found that none could hear my voice. I could only watch with sadness as my children struggled to survive.

"A few of the species evolved over the millions of years and achieved spaceflight again. Most left because this Earth was so geologically active and in an asteroid alley, which was too dangerous for their survival. I am unsure what happened to them, but three species did return. Of those that returned, only one has retained advanced technology and spaceflight, but currently, they are hiding from your species. They returned three and a half million years ago and have been searching ever since for their origins. Unlike you, they never regained the ability to hear my voice. Soon, I will introduce you to them, and through you, I will be able to talk to them again. They will be of great value in helping to prepare me for spaceflight again because of their advanced science and technology."

"Why have we not discovered this advanced species?" asked Drake.

"Humans are a dangerous and unpredictable species, so they have stayed hidden for their own protection. There are a few cultures of your species that have had contact but in a limited fashion. Over the last hundred years, they have contacted some of you humans in preparation for a full disclosure of their existence. Once your tech-nology became sufficient to understand them, they began making plans. I could watch them but not communicate mentally, so I decided to wait until such time I had a connection and felt safe. You will be introduced to them soon and act as my liaison." The voice paused to give Drake time to process what he was being told.

"Drake, my child," The voice continued, "I know this sounds like a great burden to place on your shoulders. Soon, you will have help from others of your species, and there are other species I shall soon introduce you to. Once other humans are more capable of hearing my voice, the burden will be off your shoulders. As I have mentioned, although they will be able to hear my voice, it will still be two to three generations before communication is easy for your species. Because of that, you will need to be my voice. I hear your question: '*How am I supposed to do this for generations?*' My child, before the crash, every species aboard me lived for thousands of years if they chose. With my help, you can live thousands of years. No, it is not a dream, my child, but yes, I did say thousands of years *if you choose*. The technology I possess will enable your species to choose how long they want to live.

"I feel your desire to learn and explore, and now you will have the time to learn what you have longed for. Even as a young child, your hunger for knowledge was ravenous. Soon, all that you want to learn will be available. For now, my child, I have tasks that you must help with so that we may free this ship to travel again. Your species has placed great importance on certain minerals that occur naturally on this planet. Over the last few millennia, I have gathered these minerals in large quantities, and I need your help to disperse them so that we have the financial resources to repair the ship and gather the needed materials. Drake, my child, please proceed outside the ship so that you may give detailed instructions for unloading and dispersing the minerals. Yes, child, just like we used the gold to buy this land, we have more gold and other rare minerals that need to be sold." The voice went quiet. Drake sat in the silence, turning over all the new information as he considered it. He thought about the gold, the minerals, the living one thousand years, it all seemed, well – unbe-lievable. And yet, he was here, on the spaceship, with many other sound-minded people prepared to do what was needed. He would do what was needed.

By the time Drake got outside the spaceship, one hundred robot machines had lined up, each with a large wooden box. As he inspected the boxes, he saw they contained minerals he could iden-tify, such as gold, silver, platinum, boxes of what he assumed were diamonds and rubies. Each of the boxes had a label with directions where the box was to be taken. As he looked over the boxes, Gret informed him that he was to give instructions to the drivers before they left. She reminded him that although the humans could hear some of her communication, it was still difficult, and they sometimes forgot her instructions. In the beginning, his main job was to be a teacher and guide for her children. While Gret was talking to Drake, the machines carrying the boxes started moving down the tunnel to the outside. Gret told him to go out to the trucks that were parked outside and give instructions to the drivers. When he walked down the tunnel and outside the cave, Drake found eight more trucks had arrived. The robot machines had assembled themselves by each truck.

As he walked towards the trucks, Gret was giving Drake instructions to relay to the truck drivers. Six boxes of gold were now sitting by two of the trucks. Due to the weight, they would need to be split up, 3 boxes per truck. Fourteen boxes of silver and platinum were sitting by two more trucks. The silver and platinum were much lighter, so each truck was able to carry more boxes. The remaining eighty boxes were lined up by the remaining eight trucks. Drake was wondering why the boxes were not self-levitating when Gret told him she did not want to attract too much attention at this point. *There will be a time, she said, when we want the world to know who we are and what we plan to do. For now, we have plans to conduct without interruption or questions,* Drake thought to himself. When Gret had gone quiet again, Drake took that as a sign to get the truck drivers on the move. He gathered them together and relayed Gret's instructions precisely. Once he was done giving instructions, the robots loaded the boxes onto the trucks, and the drivers drove away. Once the trucks had driven away, Gret asked Drake to come back into the ship so that she could show him his personal quarters.

As she guided him through the ship, he was trying to imagine what his personal quarters would look like inside a crystal spaceship. He heard Gret give a little laugh, "You might be surprised at your little room."

When he stepped into the room, surprise would be an understatement. The room was twenty feet by twenty feet, with a window on one side covering the wall. There was a small nook in one wall that was the bed. Next to the bed was a doorway that led to a bathroom. There was a large table in the center of the room that was five feet wide and ten feet long. There was a chair sitting in front of what he assumed was a computer terminal.

"You are correct, it is a computer." Gret confirmed.

"Where is the screen?" Drake looked around for a switch or a hidden button.

"It's holographic, you'll be able to make it whichever size you'd like." While he was still trying to imagine working with the holographic screen, she suggested he check out the view from his window. He stepped over to the window and was stunned by the sight he saw. The window looked down onto what he assumed was the flight control room for the spaceship. "You are correct," said Gret. "When we are underway at any time, you can stand in your room and watch the ship's operation. You can also block out this window for complete privacy or use it to display anything outside the ship. It will offer you a 360-degree view of the ship at any time, now or when the ship is underway. It has functions you can explore later, such as night vision, zoom, or for pure enjoyment, you could play a movie on it."

Drake thought there was not much chance he would play a movie on it but was certainly going to enjoy using it to view outside the ship. Suddenly, it dawned on him that she said *when* the ship was underway. "Yes, my son, once it is repaired and free from the inside the mountain, we will be traveling in space."

Drake could feel his heart racing at the prospect of traveling in space, especially inside this giant crystal spaceship. Gret spoke again, "Relax, child, we have repairs and teaching to do before this ship is ready to take off again. I promise you, my child, we will fly together in space. For now, it is late and time for you to get something to eat." It had been such a busy day and so exciting he had not noticed how hungry he was. She led him to the lunchroom, and when he got there, the other people from the helicopter, including the pilots, were there. Most everyone was seated at a table and eating by the time he arrived. Three were standing along the wall in front of machines like microwaves. As he walked across the room, people smiled, waved, and greeted him. On the wall next to the microwave were lookalike menus. A quick glance at the menus showed him that anything he wanted to eat was available. Drake glanced around to see where to pick up food when Gret told him to punch the number next to his selection on the menu into the machine. She told him that the machine would automatically make the selection he chose without him having to load anything into the machine. "Yes, Drake, it is exactly like the replicators they used in TV shows and movies."

After he made his selection, Drake took his meal and went to sit by the pilots from the helicopter. Gret had wanted him to sit by the pilots so he could relay information from her to them. She told him that the pilots could only hear a little of her voice, and she needed him to tell them her plans for them. Drake sat down and introduced himself to the pilots and let them know he was going to relay information from the ship. Gret Let him tell them they were to be the pilots of this spaceship. When Drake told them the plan, both men stared at him in wide wide-eyed disbelief. She had him explain to the pilots who she was and their plans to get the ship into space again. When they finished eating, Gret had him take the pilots to the flight control room of the spaceship. He explained to the pilots what their job was going to be and where they would be training. Once they were done in the control room, Drake took them to the training center. Drake explained that they would come to this room daily for their flight training. He showed them the machines they would be training at and how to put on the headgear that would relay the information into their brains. Both men were relieved they were not going to be spending months studying books and were excited about the prospect of learning to fly the ship. When they had finished in the training room, Drake led them each to their personal quarters near the flight control center and said goodnight. After dropping the men off at their personal quarters, Drake headed to his own room for the night.

Once in his room, Drake inspected it a little closer. His bathroom looked like a normal bathroom, except there were little signs in the shower, toilet, and next to the sink. The sign said that everything in the bathroom was voice-activated. All he had to do was ask the water to come on and what temperature he wanted it. To flush the toilet, all he had to do was say flush. He understood that not having on/off knobs was easier but would take a little getting used to. The bed looked amazingly comfortable, and he knew he would be sleeping in it soon. There appeared to be drawers underneath the bed, but there was nothing in them. While he was wondering about clothes, Gret informed him that he only needed to stand by the computer desk, and he could order them there. He had been in his clothes all day and had nothing to wear that night, so he decided now was a good time to try it out. She told him to stand by the desk and ask the computer to come on, which he did. She then told him to ask the computer to make him whatever clothes he required.

Drake stood in front of the terminal on the desk and asked the computer to turn on. When the computer asked what he required, Drake answered, "I need clothes, please."

The computer asked, "What clothes do you require, Drake?" He thought about it for a moment, and since he had nothing, he better ask for everything he thought he might need over the next couple of days. When he was done giving his list to the computer, a light from the computer ran up and down his body. He assumed he had just been scanned by an advanced computer technology. "Particularly good," said Gret, "I taught you well."

A buzzer sounded in the wall next to the bed nook, and then a panel slid to the side. Behind the panel was a closet with all the clothes Drake just ordered, including socks and underwear. He smiled and decided to head to bed after he changed.

4

FREEING THE SHIP

When Drake woke the next morning, he put on his new clothes and headed down to get breakfast. There were few people in the lunchroom when he got there, he waved and went over to the machine to order his breakfast. He picked up his breakfast, went over and sat at a table with four of the people. He introduced himself and they talked while they ate. Gret interrupted to ask him to come outside with the people he was sitting with at the table when they were done with their breakfast. When everyone had finished, Drake told them they were to head outside with him for a meeting. While walking outside, Gret informed him they were mining and heavy construction experts. She let him know that their job was to start excavating so they could uncover the spaceship to allow it to take off once repairs were complete. Drake relayed that information to the people and suggested that they begin meeting daily so they could produce the best plan to excavate the spaceship from inside the mountain. Gret asked him to explain to them how he could understand her, and his job was to communicate necessary information from her, they could not understand themselves. He told them that she knew they could hear her a bit and understand words and concepts but needed him to serve as an interpreter to get all the details. Gret also wanted them to begin studying in the ship's library, which would allow them more contact with her. That would lead to better communication and understanding between them. They told Drake they understood and would begin daily meetings to find the most expedient way to free the ship. Once they left Drake, Gret told him he was becoming a good leader.

"Now, my child, it is time for you to head to the flight control center to begin your lessons," said Gret. *Lessons*? Thought Drake.

"What lessons?" he asked.

"My dear child, you are the leader of my children and are the captain of this ship. Once the ship is free and ready for space travel, you must know how it operates. Yes, I am the ship, run the systems, and keep my children safe, but you will make decisions for explorations based on my recommendations. You will be picking most of the crew needed to safely run the ship in the event my systems shut down. Do not worry, my child," said Gret, "my systems run automatically even if I am down, so only a handful of my children are needed at any given time."

Aside from a quick lunch break, Drake spent the day in the flight control center, learning the ship's operations. Having Gret inside his head made learning much easier than having to read a book or sitting in class. By dinnertime, he felt confident enough that if they were in space, he could run the ship himself, the systems were so automatic. He now understood why it only took a handful of people to run the ship. By the end of the day, his anxiety about being captain of this ship was replaced by excitement looking forward to space exploration. Gret had not informed him of the plans for exploration, and he felt it was too early to ask. Instead of worrying, Drake just imagined how incredible it would be to travel in space and explore the cosmos. All his life, he wanted to go to space, and now that dream was going to become a reality once they freed the ship.

Drake spent the next two weeks fully learning the ship systems and meeting the crew members. As it turns out, the crew members had the specialized skills that were needed for space travel. There were astronomers, engineers, mechanics, electricians, a dentist, and even a doctor. Gret had informed him that within two days, more humans would be coming to the ship to join the crew. Every one of the new crew members could communicate with Gret, but in a limited fashion, which made Drake's job even more important. While Drake was eating lunch, the mining and heavy construction experts sat down with him and told him they had thought up a plan to free Gret. Once they had explained their plan to him, Gret told Drake she would have the necessary equipment brought in immediately. She also informed him she would be bringing in one hundred more humans to work on the excavation, and they could be permanent crew members if they chose. Drake was wondering what she meant by one hundred more humans, and she let him know that humans would not be the only species on the ship.

"I will explain later, child, for now, you have work to do to prepare the ship to be excavated," said Gret.

Drake spent the next two days working with the construction and mining experts to set up a plan and prepare the ship for a hundred more crew members. Gret had told him the ship could hold up to five hundred thousand individuals of varying species. She never would elaborate when she mentioned varying species, and aside from cats and dogs, he had no idea what she meant. It was in instances like this she acted like a true mother, withholding information and keeping her children motivated. Drake was in the flight control center when Gret asked him to go outside. He was only halfway down the tunnel when he could hear the sounds of heavy machinery. Once outside, he saw dozens of semi-trucks pulling trailers with heavy equipment. There were dump trucks, excavators, cranes, bulldozers, and, to his surprise, four charter buses with people in them. Gret explained she could connect with the computers to order all the equipment. She used some of the money from selling gold, silver, platinum, and precious stones to purchase the equipment needed for the excavation. It was more difficult for her to communicate mentally with the people she needed, so once she found the correct person, she had to communicate using a computer. Between the computer messages and a little bit of mental communication, she was able to convince them to come along. She told Drake it was up to him to fill them in on their plans and ask if they wanted to join the crew for space exploration when the ship was ready to leave. Drake watched as the people got off the buses and was surprised there were children with them. Gret explained the offspring of the crew had a greater ability to communicate with her than their parents. The next generation of offspring would also be better at communicating with her.

When everyone had gotten off the bus, Drake had them gather to explain what was going to be happening and where they were supposed to go on the ship inside. Everyone needed to put their personal gear into their rooms and gather in the center chamber so they could talk further about the future. He told them once they got next to the ship, there would be a computer printout with their name on it and a map of the ship, including the location of their personal room. When he finished talking to the people who had come off the buses, he went over to the individuals standing by the trucks carrying the heavy equipment. Gret told Drake that the people who were going to be operating the heavy equipment were not going to be crew members on the ship. Their job was to excavate the tunnel and the side of the mountain so the ship would be free to fly. Once their jobs were done, they would return to their normal lives. She did say that there may be half a dozen among them who had the ability to hear her may become crew members once the job was completed. Drake relayed Gret's information to the construction workers that they would be staying temporarily on the spaceship while the work was in process. He also told them there was an information packet for each one of them down by the spaceship with their construction orders, the information about the spaceship, and maps of the ship, including the rooms they would be staying in.

By the time Drake woke up the next morning and had breakfast, Gret asked him to head outside to see the progress. As he walked outside, Gret told him if her systems were up and running, she would have been able to use one of her weapon systems to carve the stone out.

"I have not been able to repair some of the systems because I lacked certain components I could not replicate. The replicators themselves are not working 100%, but they will be once we reconnect with the advanced species I told you about earlier. This species you will soon meet who came back from space three and a half million years ago has technology advanced enough to help me rebuild my systems to full capacity. Once the ship is free from the mountain, you will be introduced to them. For now, we must concentrate on excavations and education."

One hundred feet from the entrance, a barricade and a guard stopped them from going beyond. When the guard saw Drake, he called on his radio to have them stop work so Drake could proceed to the entrance. The guard handed him a hard hat, and he walked towards the entrance. Once outside, one of the men he recognized as a construction engineer came up to meet him. Drake was surprised at the amount of work that had been accomplished since the equipment just arrived the day before. When Drake mentioned that, the engineer said Gret had loaned them a few of her robots equipped with an energy beam, which was able to carve up the rocks faster than their mechanical equipment could. That meant they mostly used bulldozers, excavators, and dump trucks to remove the cut-up rock.

They were using the cut-up rock debris to build a level pad large enough to accommodate the ship once it was free from inside the mountain.

"We are cutting away half the face of the mountain to free the ship. We need all that excess material because the ship is five miles long by four miles wide and needs a hard flat pad to rest on. We are filling in a small valley to accommodate the ship. I never really thought how big the ship is," said Drake.

"I have seen it in the cave but did not realize how big it is until now. It is incredibly quite large, but weight is not really a factor because Gret keeps herself weightless, using anti-gravity," said the engineer.

"That is amazing," said Drake, "it is just like the storage boxes she uses that you can push with a finger even when they are full of heavy material."

"Absolutely correct," said the engineer. "It is too bad we could not figure out how to use that anti-gravity technology to move the material to the valley floor. We asked Gret if it would be possible to use that technology, but she said until she was repaired, it would not be possible for her to make any more than she currently has."

"How long do you think the excavation will take?" asked Drake.

"Not exactly sure, but at the rate these robots are cutting the rock, we estimate less than a month," said the engineer, "Of course, that assumes we get the twenty-five excavators and one hundred dump trucks we ordered in the next couple of days,"

"Sounds like you have everything managed here," said Drake. "Let me know if there is anything you need or have problems communicating with Gret." Drake headed back into the ship, and as before, all work stopped until he was safely inside.

Drake spent the next month studying everything he could about the ship and learning as much of the advanced science Gret could teach him. He learned the history of Gret and the species she was carrying before the crash. He was amazed at the diversity of species that were on the ship prior to the crash. Gret told him she was withholding information on the species he would soon be meeting that was still on Earth hiding from humans. She told him it would be more interesting to be surprised. Drake was in his room one afternoon when Gret asked him to go outside to see the progress of the excavation. As he walked outside the ship, he was surprised to see that the whole side of the mountain was gone.

Gret informed him that the opening was now large enough for her to fit through, but she was staying inside until more repairs were completed. She also added it was not too difficult hiding the excavation from humans, but it would be harder to hide the ship until more repairs were completed. Drake was amazed at the width of the opening and how large and smooth the level area was outside the opening. What surprised him the most was that not one piece of heavy equipment was left around the mountain. Gret told him since they were done, it was easier for her to send them away than to continue hiding them from humans until they were ready to let their presence be known.

"Now, it is time for you to be introduced to the advanced species I have told you about that is here on Earth," said Gret.

5

MEETING ONE OF THE ORIGINAL SPECIES

"Drake my child, I am calling the pilot so you can be flown by helicopter to meet the first of the species that will be traveling with us if they choose," Gret informed Drake.

"You keep saying species, Gret, I assume these are not humans," asked Drake.

"You are correct," she answered.

"Any chance you might give me a clue, who or what this species is?" he asked.

"I would prefer not," she said. "In our travels, we will be meeting incredibly different species. There will be species so different from humans you will barely recognize them as living beings. The species you will be meeting today is not so unrecognizable, and you may know what they are once you see them.

"It is important you go to this meeting without any preconceived ideas. I want you to have an open mind and know you are not in any danger today." She went quiet.

"All right, mother knows best," he said.

"That is correct," Gret said with a little laugh. "Today, you will not need any special equipment, but in the future, that will not always be the case. There will be times when you will need translating equipment. The species you will meet today speaks and understands English quite well."

"Are you telling me I will be meeting a nonhuman species that understands and speaks English?" asked Drake.

"That is correct," said Gret, "now on your way, child, your helicopter is waiting. There is a packet of papers on the helicopter that you will give to the beings you will meet. Also, once you have landed, the pilot will activate an electronic beacon to call them."

Without another question, Drake walked over and got into the waiting helicopter. This helicopter was much smaller than the one that he flew up here in and looked much faster. When he stepped inside, no other passengers were on the helicopter, just the pilot was inside. This helicopter had four passenger seats and two pilot seats. Once inside, the pilot asked him to sit beside him and handed him a pair of headphones. Once his headphones were on, the pilot started the helicopter. While the helicopter was running, the pilot told Drake they had a one-hour flight to their destination.

"Where are we flying today?" asked Drake.

"To Mount Rainier," answered the pilot.

Drake recognized the pilot from the first ride and talked to him about his experiences so far while they were flying. He also asked how the pilot liked life aboard the spaceship and the prospect of flying it in space. The pilot said he always wanted to fly and dreamed of going to space but was worried they would not pick him.

"Why is that?" asked Drake.

"To be honest, I was afraid I would fail the psych test," he answered.

"Why would you fail a psych test?"

"I knew I was a good pilot," he responded, "but I was afraid they would find out I hear voices occasionally." That confession drew a laugh from Drake.

"I bet now that you have been talking to Gret, you are not too worried about the voices you hear, are you?"

"You can say that again," said the pilot. "I spent my whole life worrying that I was crazy because I heard voices. Now, after months of living inside of her and listening to her every day, I feel normal."

"I know what you mean," said Drake.

After some silence, the pilot told Drake to get ready, "We are five minutes from our landing site."

The pilot told him they were going to be landing by a small lake near the mountain. Drake had hiked around Mount Rainier all his life, but it never flown over it in a helicopter. The sight of the mountain from the air was stunning. He looked down, saw the lake the pilot was talking about and was in awe at its unspoiled beauty. Once they landed, the pilot said he would activate the beacon.

Drake picked up the packet of paperwork and went outside to wait. He was feeling a little anxious about meeting this unknown species, and Gret spoke to him gently.

"It is about relaxing. Do not worry, my child," she said, "this is an incredibly old species. They were a space-faring race three and a half million years ago and chose to return to Earth to learn of their origins. They have watched humans for thousands of years, not knowing the connection your two species have. Today, my son, you will be answering a riddle that they have been trying to solve for over three and a half million years. Trust me, they will be incredibly grateful for the information you are carrying.

"My hope is they will come back with you to meet with me. Unlike you, they have not been able to hear me even over these last three and a half million years. I have been able to follow their evolution but unable to communicate with them. I felt it best to stay silent until such time someone like yourself was born who could hear me and communicate directly with them." She paused briefly so that Drake could process what she was explaining to him.

"My child, they have heard the beacon and are on their way here. I want you to relax. You are in no danger, they are a peaceful species and will cause you no harm." She tried to reassure him. While Drake was waiting, the pilot came out of the helicopter and stood by his side. Drake told him that Gret wanted him to be very relaxed. And to remember, the beings they were going to meet were peaceful and meant them no harm.

"Do you know what they look like?

"Not a clue," said Drake, "Gret wants us to become accustomed to meeting new species and not being afraid."

As Drake was talking to the pilot, Gret interjected, "They're coming."

Suddenly, four large hairy beings appeared to come out of the rock face directly in front of them. It honestly took all his willpower not to want to run after seeing these large hairy beings suddenly appear out of the rockface. Drake heard the pilot sharply drawing a breath but remained standing where he was. The beings walked toward Drake and the pilot at a slow, deliberate pace. He was unsure what Gret's message was in the beacon, but they did not appear upset. As the four beings walked closer, Drake realized what they were. He always thought that stories of them were nothing but folk-lore, yet here they were - four Sasquatch. The four Sasquatch stopped five feet from Drake and the pilot. Gret instructed Drake to introduce himself to the beings and say he was an emissary from Gret the spaceship.

Drake took one step forward and introduced himself to the Sasquatch. To his surprise, one of the Sasquatch stepped forward, introduced itself, and said with great expectation, "It is a pleasure to meet you." Gret had told Drake that the beings would be able to speak English, but he was surprised that these large hairy Sasquatch could speak, let alone speak English.

"Gret told us about herself and the journey our two species took together to this planet nine and a half million years ago," said the Sasquatch. "As she told you, we have searched for our origin for millions of years, and today the search is over. She also told us you can hear her voice and contact her if we have questions. As we speak, Gret is talking to our people all over the Earth through computers. This is a great day for our species and the human species. Gret has asked if we would like to come with you to meet her at the mountain."

The Sasquatch continued, "It is with great honor that we will accompany you today to meet her. Our species has three and a half million years' worth of questions for Gret, we would be grateful to come along." As the Sasquatch finished talking, the sound of a car driving quickly could be heard. Drake turned around to see what was coming just as a Jeep came around the corner into the clearing. The Sasquatch that had been speaking stepped forward past Drake and held its arm up high. The Jeep slowed down, coming to a stop twenty feet from Drake and the Sasquatch.

A blond-haired young man with light blue eyes, along with another male who appeared to be a Native American, stepped out of the Jeep and walked towards them. The Sasquatch walked toward the man and spoke to them. When they were done talking, the Sasquatch and the two men walked over to where Drake stood. The blond male had the bluest eyes Drake had ever seen and looked like he was almost seven feet tall. The other was an older male of average height. Both men were smiling but looked apprehensive. The tall, blue-eyed man stepped forward and introduced himself as Jack and the other as Bear. Shaking their hands, Drake returned the introduction.

"They told us you came from somewhere by Mount Baker to introduce yourselves to them and that you have a spaceship," said Jack. "They said that they are now in communication with the ship and are planning to visit it today. Is that true?"

"Yes, that is true," Drake confirmed. Gret then spoke to Drake and told him that Jack was the shaman for the tribe and was the liaison for his tribe to the Sasquatch. Drake told Jack the spaceship was named Gret and was a sentient spaceship.

"She said you are the shaman and liaison for your tribe," Drake said.

"I did not hear her speak," said Jack. "To be honest, very few people can hear her voice because she speaks into the mind of the people that can hear her."

Drake smiled, "Gret just told me if you would like to come meet her, She believes a closer proximity to her would enable you to talk and listen to her. She also said she noticed your body has been modified by the Sasquatch technology, which is where you get to your height. She will be pleased if you and Bear come along with the Sasquatch to meet her."

Jack looked at the Sasquatch, who shook his head, "This is a great honor to meet the mother of our species."

Bear stepped forward and said he would love to go along, but they needed to contact the tribe to let them know they were leaving. Jack looked at Bear, "It would be wonderful to have them come along."

"Greta has just informed me she has sent an email to Michelle explaining where you are going and that you would contact her after you reached the ship," Drake added.

Jack looked at Drake, "How do you know Michelle's name?"

"Well, Jack, it looks like Gret can easily read your mind, and with luck, once you get close to her, you will be able to have a conversation with her."

While they were talking, a man came out of the rockface the Sasquatch had come out of and walked towards the group. Drake looked at Jack, "Gret talked to his uncle Mick and let him know what was going on, and he was coming to tell you it was all right."

Mick came over, introduced himself and shook Drake's hand.

"I have spoken to Gret over the computer," said Mick. "It would be advantageous for Jack and Bear to go meet her. This is a great opportunity to learn about human and Sasquatch history and where we came from. She said that Mount Rainier somehow blocks her ability to communicate fully. She thinks once Jack is near her, he should easily be able to communicate with her."

Drake nodded enthusiastically, "That would be wonderful!" Plus, he was sure Jack and Bear would enjoy meeting her. "Jack, Gret just informed me Michelle has replied and will let everyone in the tribe know where you two went. Also, Michelle told her to have Lobo write her tonight, or she would not cook him dinner for two weeks."

Bear nudged Jack's shoulder and said, "Looks like we are going for a helicopter ride, Lobo!" He gave a wild grin.

Jack laughed and looked at Drake, "Do you have all the clothes and gear we need to hold us over for a few days?"

Drake nodded, "The ship will provide anything you need, all you need to do is ask."

Bear looked at Jack curiously, "What do you mean?"

"You will learn more once you get there, but Gret is a sentient spaceship over nine and a half million years old. She is what brought all our human and Sasquatch ancestors to Earth. She can provide everything you need."

"The helicopter holds four passengers, so Jack, Bear and two of the Sasquatch can go," said the pilot.

The four Sasquatch talked to each other and decided who would go.

"I was worried the helicopter would have trouble carrying four of you big guys," said the pilot, looking at the Sasquatch.

One of the Sasquatch smiled at the pilot, "We were thinking the same thing."

"Well," Drake clapped his hand on the helicopter, "it is time to get going. Gret said she is excited to meet you all."

"Drake, didn't you say that Gret was a computer inside the spaceship?" Bear furrowed his eyebrows.

"Bear, Gret is the spaceship, and she is completely self-aware," said Drake. "She is extremely intelligent, feels love and sadness, and has a great sense of humor." He added. "Over the last nine and a half million years, she felt great loneliness and sadness watching the species on her struggle and sometimes die. In every sense of the word, she has been and is the mother of all the species she cared for. Once all of you communicate with her the first time, you will fully understand," He glanced at everyone anxiously. "She just told me we are dilly-dallying too long. We need to get on our way so that she can greet you."

"Well, she certainly sounds like my mother did," Mick burst out with a laugh, "so you all better get on your way, guys, before she spanks you." That comment drew a smile from everyone, and they headed into the helicopter to go meet Gret. The pilot instructed the two Sasquatch to sit in the forward passenger seats to balance the weight. Their weight was one thing, but the helicopter was not designed to carry someone over seven feet tall. Bear gave a little chuckle and said he was grateful he was not very tall, and teased Jack because even he was almost hitting the ceiling of the helicopter like the Sasquatch. When they were all seated, the pilot handed out headsets to the passengers, including two special ones that were designed specifically for the Sasquatch.

Once underway, Jack speculated, "It might have been easier and faster to take one of our large drones."

The pilot glanced back at him, "What were the drones like?"

"They are large, supersonic, and can fly into space," Jack mentioned casually.

"Oh my, I am hoping you let me fly one of those drones sometimes," said the pilot.

"Did you say they can fly into space?"Drake said with excitement, "If so, I am up for a ride also," he added. He went quiet briefly as though listening to someone. "Gret just told me we sound like a bunch of kids on the playfield." He laughed.

"I guarantee I would feel like a kid if I could fly one of those drones," the pilot laughed as well.

"You should have seen Jack the first time he flew into space," Bear tapped Jack on the shoulder playfully. "He was the true definition of a happy kid playing," he added.

"I must admit," said Drake, "I am sure I will be acting like a kid flying in space the first time."

With all the talking, the trip went by quickly. The pilot landed the helicopter facing the mountain. The face had been cut away, so when the dust had settled, they had a clear view of the huge spaceship inside. When Drake had said Gret was a spaceship, he never explained how large the ship was. The silence from the passengers inside the helicopter showed how stunned they were at the sight of Gret. Bear was the first to speak, and all he uttered was, "Oh my God, I had no idea. The ship is the size of a mountain."

"Yes, she is," replied Jack, "Looks like she is approximately five miles long and four miles wide.

"I cannot believe we have not detected the spaceship in the last three and a half million years," said a Sasquatch.

"Gret has been hiding until someone could communicate with her."

"I am amazed that with our technology we could not detect her," said the Sasquatch. "It looks as though we both have advanced science we will be sharing back and forth," it added. "Gret said she is currently masking the excavation from humans until she is ready to announce her presence. We have the technology to hide from humans, but Gret's Is much greater than our own. Our species has much to learn from her. I am amazed at her ability to cloak herself." The Sasquatch surveilled the ship. "Even with our advanced technology, we could not cloak an area the size of this mountain that Gret has."

Drake spoke up. "Gret has mentioned she has science to teach, which you will find much more impressive than the ability to hide this mountain. She enjoyed watching your species evolve in advance to space-fairing technology. In your three and a half million years of space exploration, Gret said you never achieved faster-than-light travel. You will be quite interested in her interstellar drive. She said it allows her to travel hundreds of millions of times faster than the speed of light. Using her interstellar drive, Gret said, you will be able to find all your species that are scattered throughout the star systems in a matter of months."

"We would be grateful for the ability to contact our species," said the Sasquatch. "Our people left but never came back. Thus we have a great interest in what happened to them and where they went," it added.

"When you come into the ship, she will be glad to show you the interstellar drive and anything else that you are interested in," said Drake.

"Now that we are standing close to Gret," said Jack, "I can hear some of her words."

"Gret can also hear you better now," Drake smiled. "Once we are inside the ship, communication will be much easier," he added.

"Once we are on the ship, anyone that cannot hear her may talk to her through a computer. Gret has noticed some are hungry and suggests we go to the lunchroom and have something to eat before we tour the ship."

"Well, I don't know about anyone else," said Jack, "but I am more than ready to eat."

"When are you not ready to eat?" Bear rolled his eyes.

"Gret asked me to inform our two Sasquatch family members that she can meet their dietary requirements," said Drake. "Jack, I think you will enjoy the lunchroom. You can access it twenty-four hours a day and order anything you can think of."

"Well then, what is the holdup?" said Jack, "My stomach's calling!" With that comment, everyone started heading towards the ship.

The first thing Jack noticed when they got to the lunchroom was an oversized table that had not been there before.

"Gret, you amaze me," he said to her.

"Compliments will get you everywhere, my child," she said. "As we gather the different species, we will be opening more and some quite different lunchrooms," she added. "There are aquatic species that will be traveling with us, and you can imagine the type of lunchrooms they will need."

"You are bringing aquatic species?" asked Jack.

"Yes, my child," she answered, "there are species that have evolved enough to bring along on our journey. Dolphins and porpoises are just two of the species we will be bringing along. Once we contact them, I will be able to communicate directly with them and let them know of our intentions to return to space. If they choose, they, too, can return to space and explore. They are highly intelligent but have also lost the ability to communicate with me. Humans have been studying them for decades, but their language is too complicated for humans to understand. Once they have been outfitted with translators, everyone will be able to talk to them.

"Drake, even though they do not possess the technology, their minds are brilliant, and as you have seen, they are quite playful. What you may find most interesting is that their mathematical ability is greater than that of humans, even without computers. Their spatial mathematical ability makes them great navigators, especially in space," said Gret. "Now, my child, time for you to show these hungry beings how to work the lunchroom."

After Drake gave the new guests a rundown of the lunchroom and everyone had their food, they sat down and talked. Once everyone was seated, he explained that after they ate, they would head to the flight control room, then to one of the learning centers, and finally be shown to their quarters. The pilot started asking Jack more about the drone that could fly in space. Jack told him that if it were OK with Gret, he would have one flown to the ship so that he could try it out. With a little chuckle, Gret told Jack to tell him it would be fine to have one flown over so he could try it. When Jack relayed the information, the pilot acted like a little kid at Christmas and could barely contain his excitement. The pilot explained he knew he was going to be able to fly in space in the big ship but was afraid it could be months or years before they took off. Being able to fly the drone into space was now his absolute life dream.

"It looks like you and Jack will get along quite well because he acted the same way the first time he flew into space in the drone." Bear shared.

One of the Sasquatch looked at the pilot, "You might enjoy piloting one of our underwater ships in our caverns."

"Underwater ships," said the pilot, "what are those?"

"We have underground caverns all over this world," said the Sasquatch, "and needed a vehicle to travel between them at a high rate of speed."

"How fast are you talking?" asked the pilot.

"They can travel at hypersonic speeds over twenty times the speed of sound, if necessary," said the Sasquatch. "If required, they can also fly into outer space."

"With all this new technology, I feel like I have died and gone to heaven," said the pilot.

"Gret just told me, in the past, every species has their own special gift, which made our family strong," said Jack.

Bear glanced around, "It looks like everyone is done eating, I, for one, would like to see the flight Control Center. Who is with me?"

"Looks like someone else is acting like a young child at Christmas," said Jack.

"Just a little," said Bear. "You know I like technology, and I am looking forward to what a flight Control Center looks like in a spaceship five miles long," he added.

"I just heard Gret laugh a little bit," said Jack.

"She did laugh a little," said Drake, looks like she was right, once in the ship, you would hear her better. "She said once you spend time in her learning center, your ability to hear her will increase."

"I would like to know if the different species on the ship can also hear each other's thoughts," asked Jack. "Michelle and I can hear each other's thoughts."

"Gret says yes," answered Drake. "Many of the original species on the spaceship were able to communicate mentally with one another, she said. It was especially helpful when aquatic species and land species wanted to communicate."

"Well at least I know Michelle and I are not crazy," said Jack.

"I do not know about that," said Bear, "maybe just a little."

"Well, now I know Gret has a sense of humor because I just heard her laugh," said Jack.

"She has a great sense of humor," said Drake, "but she is very much like a mother. She just told me it is time to get to the flight control room," added Drake.

"At least she cannot spank us," said Bear as he hurried out the door.

As expected, everyone was amazed at the flight control center. Drake explained all the equipment inside the flight Control Center. After spending two months learning the ship's operation, he had become an expert on all its controls. Gret had made sure he knew how to run every aspect of the ship in the event she was not able to. Everyone was amazed at the lack of physical controls needed to operate the ship. Jack explained that in the past, all operations and commands were accomplished by mental communication. He informed them that Gret would be adding manual command stations until such time operators could communicate fully mentally.

"Gret has asked me to inform you that much of the ship's piloting will be from the aquatic section," said Jack.

"How is that possible," asked the pilot, "will I be wearing a scuba suit?"

"No," said Jack, "*you* will be piloting from this room."

"Glad to hear that," the pilot looked relieved, "because I cannot swim too well."

"Grateful to hear that also," one of the Sasquatch chimed in, "because we do not swim at all."

"Gret wanted you all to know most of the piloting in the future will be accomplished by dolphins and porpoises."

"How are fish going to be able to pilot a spaceship?" asked Bear.

"First," said Drake, "porpoises and dolphins are mammals. Secondly, porpoises and dolphins are highly intelligent, and their mathematical ability is greater than humans or even Sasquatch. Gret said their advanced mathematical abilities and high intelligence make them the perfect pilots traveling in space. She wants you to know once we have them on board, her translator will allow you to speak to them.

"At this point, there are none that she can communicate mentally with, but once they have translators, she will be able to communicate with them. She added that it will also take them a couple of generations to communicate mentally with her. Gret wants me to inform you all, it is getting late, and time for you to be shown to your personal quarters." Drake turned and headed towards the door.

"Most definitely sounds like my mom," said Bear, following Drake out of the flight control room.

Drake picked up an information packet for everyone as he left the room. He informed everyone that they would all meet for breakfast and review their individual plans for their stay on the ship. Jack asked if he could talk to Drake after everyone else had been dropped off at their room.

"I am simply curious if you ever get used to hearing Gret's voice in your head?" Jack asked in a hushed voice.

Drake smiled encouragingly, "She has been in my head my whole life, so I am used to it. I honestly think it will not take you exceptionally long to get used to her." He put his hand on Jack's shoulder. "In fact, if I go too long without hearing her, I feel a little lonely," Drake added.

"Well, I am kind of worried how Michelle would react with Gret in my head all the time," said Jack.

Gret's voice cut through, "Not to worry, my child, I know when and when not to listen or invade personal time."

Drake nodded in agreeance. "Also, from what you said about your ability to communicate mentally with Michelle, Gret believes she will be able to hear her voice once she is here."

"I could hear every word," said Jack. "You are right, Drake, she is just like a mother. Although my mom could not listen to my thoughts," Jack smiled. "The best part about Gret is it whenever you have a question, you can ask, and she will answer. Homework must have been easy with Gret in your head."

"You are right about that, Jack. There were times when I had a professor disagree with me, and she was able to give me the page or paragraph of a book to prove him wrong," said Drake.

"I could have used that a couple of times in high school," said Jack. "Well, I should hit the hay. See you in the morning, Drake!"

"Night, Jack!" Drake headed down the hall towards his quarters before turning back, "Oh! If you have any questions, use your comm-link to call me."

At breakfast the next morning, everyone in the new group was talkative. The two Sasquatch said they were excited about going to look at the ships faster than light drive systems. They explained that since their ancestors had returned from space exploration three and a half million years ago, they have been trying to develop faster than the light propulsion system. They told the group that they are very community-oriented, and their greatest desire is to find their kind that never returned from space.

"It is of great importance for us to find and reconnect with our kind that spread throughout the solar systems. We are positive that none of them achieved faster than light drive themselves, or they would have already returned to us. We have calculated it will only take us a few months to a decade to search the surrounding solar systems using Gret's propulsion system to find them." The Sasquatch said.

"Would you mind if I tagged along?" The pilot asked.

"We would be pleased if you came along." They smiled at him.

"The fastest I have ever flown was in a jet," said the pilot, "and I am curious what the propulsion system looks like."

"I think you will be surprised at how simple this ship's propulsion system is and how small it is," said Jack. "I am looking forward to talking to you about it over dinner, though Gret just told me I am minimizing such an amazing scientific achievement by saying how small and simple it is."

"I am interested in learning how the replicators work," said Bear. "Gret told me last night that the replicators draw the material they use from the air and surrounding materials. She told me that in space, they also draw the material needed as they are flying. These replicators could end world hunger here on Earth if they were available to everyone." He let that sink in before he continued on.

"The most amazing thing she told me was that you could use one replicator to build the parts to make another replicator."

"Gret would like me to say you are a selfless human Bear," said Drake. Jack started smiling, then laughing lightly at that last sentence.

"I heard it too," said Bear, "but it was not that funny."

Jack started laughing a little harder, "Gret just told me, 'grow up, child.'"

"That seriously sounds like something Gret would have told me," said Drake.

When Jack stopped laughing, he asked if it would be OK to hang around with Drake for the day because he had so many questions.

"That sounds like fun," said Drake. "I have spent the last two months studying and working around the ship and could use a day relaxing," he added. "The ship is huge, so it looks like a chance for us to grab a couple electric scooters and take a tour."

"You are a man after my own childish heart," Jack placed his hand on his chest. "How fast are these scooters, Drake?" he asked.

"Not sure," said Drake. "Since there are not many people on the ship, we might have a chance to find out unless mom stops us," he quipped.

Both Drake and Jack started laughing loudly after the last comment.

"Did your mom just yell at you two young boys?" asked Bear.

"Yes," they replied in unison, "she said grow up, have fun, but be careful."

"Looks like you two are cut from the same cloth," said a Sasquatch. "Jack, I have watched you your whole life, and you have always been a playful kid, do not fully grow up!" It gave a kind smile.

"All right, looks like we all have our day planned, see you at dinner time," said Drake.

When the group met for dinner, one of the Sasquatch announced that they would open an entrance to the cavern network outside the field near the mountain base.

"Do you have a network of caverns?" asked Jack.

"Yes," replied the Sasquatch, "Two million years ago, we built a network of caverns around the world for protection. There were objects hitting the Earth from space that damaged our cities and killed or injured our species. We built caverns deep underground to protect our species and other species on Earth, including humans. There are over four hundred thousand interconnecting caverns around the world that can be accessed by hidden shafts around the world. Each is hundreds of miles long and is self-contained, with food, water, and a light source.

"We were planning to acknowledge our presence to humans in the next few years because of astronomical events that will occur soon and could harm humans living on the surface of the Earth.

There will be a burst of energy coming from a nearby galaxy, which will potentially damage human DNA. This event happens every 200,000 years and each time, we have ushered humans into our caverns to protect them. Now that Gret has revealed herself and her plan, it will be easier to connect with humans. It would also be good to have easy access to the underwater hypersonic crafts. Our pilot friend said he would enjoy flying one into outer space. It would make him happy. It would also be a great way for him to practice piloting in space before he gets to pilot Gret."

"What exactly are these hypersonic crafts used for?" asked Bear.

"They are used to travel throughout the underground cavern system," said the Sasquatch. He launched into a deeper explanation, "We have not wanted the humans to know of our existence for fear they will try to harm us. Our species live in the caverns around the world, and these crafts allow us to travel unseen. Up until the last two centuries, we were known to humans and sometimes worked side by side with their cultures.

"Recently, human technology has reached a level that could harm us, so we have stayed hidden. We have many humans living and collaborating with us currently. Throughout the world, if we find a human that has been injured, we bring them into our society, and they live with us in harmony. In the past, the humans were allowed to go back to their society once they were healed. In the last few centuries, we have had to keep humans with us for fear they would let our presence be known too dangerous humans.

"As I said, we are about to let our presence be known to the humans and have been working towards that goal in various locations around the Earth. Over the past century, we have been educating humans to help us with this goal. Jack and Bear have been working with us for years, using our technology to make the Earth a healthier environment. The hypersonic craft will allow our species to safely contact the human governments when it is time. Crafts will also be necessary to transport our species to Gret.

"It is time for our species to come aboard Gret and begin making repairs so she may fly again. Thousands have expressed their desire to come aboard to prepare for the future journeys. Gret has also told us we may now outfit our own spaceships with the faster-than-light drives and begin searching for our kind before she is ready for her first flight. Within days, we shall have a large shaft entrance completed outside. Once it is ready, hundreds of the Sasquatch species will arrive to begin work. Many of the humans that had been working with us have also decided to come along. Most of those have expressed a desire to journey with Gret because they have no living relatives on Earth. Our technology has allowed humans to live more than twice the age they normally would, which is why they have no living relatives left. My species was grateful to learn that Gret's technology will allow all species to live for as long as they choose. Our species has a great desire to learn, and living indefinitely is a gift that will allow us to learn even more. Our pilot friend will be flying us back to our mountain today to rejoin our species. It has been a great pleasure to meet you all and connect with our mother, Gret."

"I will be traveling back with the Sasquatch," Jack spoke up. "Michelle said she would like to come here and spend time learning about Gret and our human history," he added.

"That sounds great," said Drake, "looking forward to meeting her. Bringing Michelle here, it sounds like you may be planning to stay longer than you had planned."

"My thoughts exactly," said Jack. When we come back, we will be flying one of our large drones. It would be nice to have something faster than a helicopter to do some of the work we are going to need to in the future."

"Will this be one of the drones that can fly into space?" asked Drake.

"Absolutely," said Jack. "I figured you and our pilots would enjoy flying in it, especially if we took a quick trip into space."

"You know I would," said Drake, "looking forward to my first ride into space. Looks like between you and the Sasquatch, we will have plenty of fast toys around here soon. Gret told me to tell you all, 'See you all soon, and have safe travels, my children.'"

"I will be staying for a couple more weeks before going home. I still have plenty more work to do preparing to distribute replicators," said Bear. "I will be seeing you all when you come back."

6

SASQUATCH SHOW THE HUMANS
THEIR CAVERNS

Drake was relaxing in his quarters when Gret told him to head outside to meet the visitors. He asked her who it was, and she told him to head outside and be surprised for once. Once outside the ship, he saw a large semicircular aircraft landing on the pad. It was the size of a football field and did not sound as it landed. At first, Drake thought it was a UFO until he saw Jack walk out with a lady by his side, followed by their pilot friend. Drake met them in the field, and Jack introduced him to Michelle. After their greeting, Michelle told him she thought she heard Gret telling her hello.

Drake paused, "Gret just told me that is exactly what she did."

"This is marvelous," said Michelle, "I thought Jack was just kidding me."

"Michelle," Jack gently touched her arm, "Gret said once you are closer to her, you two should be able to communicate a little better. She also said if you spend time in the learning center, she believes you should be able to communicate better than most."

"This is extremely exciting," gushed Michelle. "Jack and I can communicate mentally, but this is the first time being able to do it with someone else. Are you really telling me Gret is the ship rather than a person?" asked Michelle.

"As unbelievable as it sounds, Gret is the ship you see inside the mountain," said Drake.

"I am looking forward to meeting her and having great conversations," said Michelle.

"Gret said she feels the same way, Michelle. She also just informed me that we are having other visitors arriving in a few minutes."

No sooner than Drake had finished talking, then they heard a sound near the ship that Jack and Michelle had just landed in.

"Gret said we need to stay here for a few minutes until the ground stabilizes," said Drake.

While they were looking out onto the pad where the noise was coming from, an area of the pad started glowing blue. They watched the blue, glowing ground disappear and become a two-hundred-foot circular hole. There was no explosion, no dust, no debris whatsoever. Suddenly, there was just a hole where the ground had been. The area around the hole now looked like a circular clear glass plate. As they continued watching, something slowly came out of the hole. A glossy, ebony-black shape began emerging from the hole. When it was completely out of the hole, it became apparent it was some sort of flying craft. It was completely black and shaped like a futuristic three-hundred-foot-long jet fighter or spaceship. After it came out of the hole, it hovered silently fifty feet above the ground for a few seconds, then slowly settled onto the ground. Drake saw no windows or doors; the unknown craft was simply black and shiny.

"What is that?" asked Michelle.

"I am not sure," said Drake, "Do you have any ideas, Jack?"

"Not a clue," answered Jack. As they watched, a small opening appeared on the side of the craft, and a ramp slowly slid out to the ground.

A group of twelve Sasquatch came out of the craft and walked down the ramp. Two humans, a man and a woman, followed the Sasquatch down the ramp next. Following the first two humans down the ramp was a human male who looked to be as tall as a Sasquatch and what Drake assumed was a Sasquatch female. Lastly came a human male who was barely over five feet tall. That ship looks incredible, said the pilot. I bet that is one of those hypersonic crafts the Sasquatch were talking about, he added. The Sasquatch and the four humans walked toward where Drake, Jack and Michelle were standing. Even though Drake had seen the other two Sasquatch, the sight of twelve walking together amazed him. He had a difficult time telling the difference between them because they looked so similar and were all over seven feet tall.

The pilot spoke, "I truly hope that is one of the hypersonic crafts, and they are going to let me pilot it. Soon."

The new Sasquatch and humans approached Drake, Michelle, and Jack.

"Greetings," said the lead Sasquatch, "Gret has informed us that you are called Drake. We are most pleased to meet you. From the looks of the other ship, we must assume that this is Jack and his partner Michelle. Forgive us, but we monitored your transmissions as you flew here." The Sasquatch then looked at the pilot, "We would be honored if you would fly our craft soon. Our hearing is exceptional, and we heard your conversation as we were approaching."

"I look forward to flying your craft soon," said the pilot.

The couple that had followed the Sasquatch out of the craft stepped forward and introduced themselves.

"Name is Raymond," said the man, "and this is my wife, Stella."

Then the tall human that followed the couple out stepped forward to introduce himself and the two with him.

"My name is Doug. The little guy here is called Mike, and this tall gal is called Daru."

Drake introduced himself, then Michelle and Jack to the group.

"It is wonderful to meet you," said Drake, "and Gret is quite excited to meet you all."

"Our Sasquatch friends told us that Gret is the spaceship we see inside the mountain. Is that correct?" asked Doug.

"That is correct," said Drake, "She is the spaceship but much more. She is a sentient, self-aware computer that, simply put, is the mother of all of us standing here. She informed me that you will receive a history lesson once you are settled inside."

"Gret has asked us to bring these humans to her," said the Sasquatch. "These are a few of the humans that have been helping my species so that we may more easily integrate with your species." He gestured to the tall female who was with them. "She is what you would call a hybrid of human and Sasquatch. It is common for our species to become partners, and there are instances when they have offspring. The small human, called Mike, has been with our species for decades and has a Sasquatch partner."

"It is nice to meet you all," said Drake, "let me take you inside and show you to your personal quarters. Once you are settled into your quarters, I will meet you in the lunchroom."

When they got to the ship, each of the new guests was given a personal packet containing maps and all the necessary information about the ship. By the time Drake got to the lunchroom, all the new guests were there sitting and eating. The twelve Sasquatch, Daru, the hybrid female, and Doug, the tall human, all sat at a special table built for tall species. Mike, the small human, was sitting with Raymond, his wife Stella, Jack, Michelle, and the pilot at a table adjacent to the larger one.

Michelle looked up at Drake when he got to the tables, "This ship is incredible. It is amazing because I can hear Gret talking occasionally."

"I am glad to hear that," said Drake. "Gret just told me she is looking forward to you visiting the Learning Center. You will be able to use computers to communicate with her, and you should also be able to hear her better in there."

"I, for one, am glad to be back," said Jack, "because now I do not have to rely on Michelle for all my meals."

"Keep it up, smart boy, and I will not do any more cooking for you," Michelle teased.

"I do not know about anyone else," said Mike, "but I really like these replicators for my lunches. I have been living with the

Sasquatch for a long time and did not realize how much I missed a good steak because they eat mostly fruits and vegetables."

"I don't know, you better watch out, I heard steak stunts your growth," said Doug. The twelve Sasquatch got a nice chuckle out of that last line. "The Sasquatch's nickname for Mike is 'goat'. I will explain that later to you, Drake," Doug added. That made the Sasquatch laugh even more.

After watching the Sasquatch laugh, Drake said, "I am looking forward to that conversation!"

After everyone had finished their lunch, Drake asked the Sasquatch if it was possible to get a tour of their caverns in their fantastic ship. He explained that Gret said she could not get a clearer picture of the inside of the caverns because of the incredibly dense crystal and gold walls. The pilot asked if he could go along since riding in the hypersonic craft would be wonderful.

Stella responded, "She did not know much about the science of the caverns, but they were beautiful inside. You will not believe how incredible the berries and fruit inside them taste."

Michelle and Jack agreed they would enjoy a tour of the caverns. "Especially if we get to ride in that incredible ship," said Jack.

Mike, Doug, and Daru decided to stay and take a tour of Gret while the rest toured the cavern. Raymond said he and Stella were also going to stay on Gret and do some studying in the learning center themselves.

"I am interested in the technology built into this ship," said Raymond, "and would like to learn a lot more. Stella and I are trying to decide whether we would like to go on the journey when Gret takes off. We want to spend time here and learn more before we decide."

One of the Sasquatch spoke and said it would be an honor to take them all on a tour of their caverns. "We might even have a few moments for our young pilot here to operate the craft for a while."

The pilot gave a hoot at that, "Count me in then!"

"When everyone is done with their meal, you can meet me at our craft," said the Sasquatch before getting up and leaving.

"Well, it looks like we are going on the ride of our lives," said Drake. Fifteen minutes later, everyone was waiting outside next to the ramp into the Sasquatch's Hypersonic craft. After everyone was assembled at the base of the craft's ramp, the Sasquatch stepped out onto the ramp, asking them to please come inside. Everyone laughed as the pilot ran up the ramp into the craft. Except for the door opening, there did not appear to be any other openings or windows in the craft from the outside. Once inside the craft, it was apparent there was a row of five-foot-tall windows down each side, which was only visible from the inside.

The craft was three hundred feet long, and the interior was divided into three sections. The piloting area was at the front and had seating for twenty people, including two pilots. The center section had a mixture of large and small padded chairs, With small tables between each one. There were ten large couches facing the windows on the side. The section in the back contained a dining room, kitchen, and restrooms, which included showers and lockers. The Sasquatch suggested the pilot take the seat next to him, and if everyone else would like to, they could ride up front so he could explain what they were seeing. Everyone agreed to sit up front, and once they were seated, the Sasquatch lifted the craft off the ground.

The craft was silent as it began moving. Once the craft lifted off the ground, it turned around, tilted downwards, and slowly went down into the shaft. The Sasquatch explained they built this shaft today to allow the craft access to the surface.

"Normally, shafts are built for smaller vehicles or foot traffic," explained the Sasquatch. "It is rare we build a shaft large enough for the crafts to come out to the surface because we do not want humans to detect us. Gret told us that she would be able to hide our craft from the humans, so we built a larger shaft this time. Our cavern at this location is two miles underground below Gret's mountain, yet with her superior masking, we were unable to locate her until she let us." Thirty seconds after they left the surface, the craft flew out into a huge cavern. The passengers all were stunned at the immense size of the cavern.

Drake looked around in awe, "When you said cavern, I expected a small tunnel, not a two-mile-wide opening with a lake in the center."

"These caverns were meant for habitation, especially in an emergency," said the Sasquatch. "Each cavern has a light at the top that can grow the plants on either side. It also has a night-day cycle, which imitates the sun's natural twelve-hour night and day-cycle. As Stella said earlier, the plants growing on either side of the cavern are edible and good tasting. Now, if you do not mind, we are going to be going underwater, and we will be traveling at a high rate of speed. The water is one mile wide and one mile deep. We can achieve our high rate of speed underwater because of a forcefield around the craft, which will not allow the water to touch the outside hull."

The Sasquatch flew the craft into the water and down to a depth of twenty feet. Once to depth, the craft began to accelerate rapidly without any sound or feeling of movement. As they were accelerating, the Sasquatch informed them that, at top speed, the craft could circle the Earth in less than two hours. Each cavern was three hundred miles long, which meant it took under two minutes to go through each cavern. The higher speeds were too fast for any species to operate manually, so computers piloted the ships once they got underway.

"I am grateful for that," the pilot said with relief, "because I cannot imagine flying underwater at 15,000 miles an hour."

"The speed is so fast, mostly, what you see are lights and shadows as we are traveling." After ten minutes of going full speed, the Sasquatch announced they were slowing down and were going to stop at a cavern. When the craft stopped, it surfaced and the Sasquatch asked them to come outside with him. Once outside the craft, they saw small structures scattered alongside the cavern walls going up the tiers. "Those are homes for residents of this cavern," said the Sasquatch. "In this cavern, we have approximately two thousand Sasquatch and fifty humans living and working together. You will notice the plants around the homes and covering the terraces are tall and well-formed. All the food the residents of this cavern need to survive is grown in the cavern. The residents have plenty of room between the buildings, which gives them privacy."

The Sasqatched launched into an explanation, "The caverns are three hundred miles long, two miles wide, and two miles from the lake bottom to the cavern top. The land on each side of the lake is half a mile from the water to the cavern wall, but due to terracing, there is twice as much land to cultivate crops. Each cavern can comfortably sustain one hundred thousand individuals indefinitely, and twice that if necessary. For comfort and to maintain privacy, we try to keep the number of inhabitants down to 20,000 per cavern.

"There are over three hundred thousand caverns around the Earth at different depths. These caverns can easily support the entire human population many times over, with plenty of room for the other sentient species Gret has informed us of. There also is plenty of land to support those nonsentient species that might be at risk. The lakes inside the caverns can support all the sentient aquatic species and the food supply they require. The lakes are one mile wide and one mile deep and, in total, contain more freshwater than is on the surface. One hundred thousand of the caverns contain saltwater lakes, which are required for certain aquatic species to survive. Most of the saltwater species will suffer no damage from the astronomical event and will not need to be relocated.

"There are multiple shafts in each cavern that go to the surface. These are used to transport individuals and materials into and out of the cavern. I thought you would be interested to know that in the 15 minutes traveling in the craft, we went from Mount Baker in Washington state two directly under Manhattan Island, in New York on the East Coast. The shaft at this location comes out inside the basement of a building on Manhattan Island. Humans primarily use it to do in-person banking and traveling. The Sasquatch do not use shafts that come out in a human species-occupied environment. Once Gret has Informed the human governments of her existence, the Sasquatch shall join her in the announcement of our existence."

"I do not know," said the pilot, "I have been in New York, and I am not sure they would be overly surprised if you were walking down the street."

"I think Gret was laughing," said Michelle.

"She was," Drake confirmed, "Gret knows how humans think and said she agrees with the pilot. Not many people in New York would pay the least bit of attention if a Sasquatch were walking down the sidewalk."

"You might be right," said the Sasquatch, "but it is not wise to take a chance. Now it is time we head back to Gret because we have a lot of work to do ahead of us."

On the way back, the Sasquatch showed the pilot how to set the computer for the trip back. The Sasquatch told the pilot, "From now on, you will be able to take this craft anywhere throughout the caverns, and your next lesson will be how to pilot it in outer space."

"My life has been a blessing since I met Gret, and now you are making all my dreams come true," said the pilot.

"Gret said her dreams have also come true," Drake told the Sasquatch. "Finally seeing inside of the caverns is wonderful and knowing they can protect all her children gives her comfort."

As the craft slowly flew out of the cavern and landed in the field next to Gret's mountain, Drake informed them it would be dinner time soon.

"Gret suggests that everyone headed to their personal quarters to rest up for dinner because you have had a long day of travel."

"I am not too tired from traveling," said Jack, "but I should rest up for dinner."

"You and your stomach have a better reputation than we do," said Michelle. "Gret just told me all boys are the same, all they can think about is food and play."

"Oh, come on," said Jack, "you know I am a growing boy."

"Yes, and you are going to start growing bigger in the tummy if you keep eating like that," said Michelle.

"Even the young boys of my species eat ravenously for the first hundred years," said the Sasquatch. "Looks like Jack will get good use of the replicator."

"I should ask Gret to remove the replicator from our room so Jack does not spend all his time eating," said Michelle.

"I do not spend all my time eating, I work out and study also," said Jack.

"Yes, you work out your arms lifting forks to your mouth, and study what next to eat off the menu," replied Michelle, with a big grin.

"Jack do not let them tease you too much," said Drake, "Food always sounds good to me, too."

"Gret just said, time for the kids to quit playing and get moving, or nobody gets dessert," said Jack.

"She sounds very much like a mother," said the Sasquatch as they walked towards Gret.

At dinner, the Sasquatch informed Drake they had compiled a list of components needed to complete repairs to Gret. They estimated it would take two weeks to complete repairs, most of which was manufacturing the new parts.

"Much of the damage was in areas that Gret's machines could not access, which is why she was unable to inspect or repair them. Much of the damaged areas that need repair are too small for Sasquatch to access, so we will use our skilled humans to complete the repairs. Gret has informed us that she looks forward to the repairs being completed and bringing more of her children on board," said the Sasquatch.

"Gret just told me," said Jack, "this is the happiest she has been in nine and a half million years."

"That she feels like a mother watching her children play in the yard," he added. The Sasquatch told the pilot they would be honored if he would fly one of the crafts bringing parts and more of Gret's children.

"You do not have to ask me twice," said the pilot. "My life has changed, and I do not think even Gret is any happier than I am." The mood in the lunchroom was happy, and everyone talked long after dinner. The next two weeks were the busiest since Drake had boarded Gret. Another one hundred Sasquatch came aboard to work on Gret. With the Sasquatch came fifty humans who had been living and working with the Sasquatch. Most of the parts needed to repair Gret were modified from Sasquatch spaceships and equipment. Gret's vast library and detailed schematics allowed them to manufacture the remaining components needed for her repair.

The humans in the Sasquatch worked side by side, repairing and installing new components into Gret. Drake noticed that the pilot was one of the happiest people in the group. Whenever he had a chance, he would fly either one of the Sasquatch craft or human-built drones. He never seemed to tire from the flying, and on multiple occasions, he got to fly into outer space. Drake was lucky enough to fly with him on two occasions into space. Gret was quite amused on one occasion when they turned off the artificial gravity, and they got to float around. She told them that they were just like Jack, two little boys that all they wanted to do was eat and play.

"I work too," Drake told her, laughing as he and Jack rode electric scooters in the ship's hallways. She told him that once they were in space, she would turn off the artificial gravity when he and Jack were riding their scooters too fast on the ship. Gret told him that while her systems were being repaired, her heart was healed as well by having her children back on board. "For nine and a half million years, I watched, unable to do anything to help my children, and now I feel whole again."

7

MOVING GRET OUTSIDE

E xactly two weeks after beginning repairs, the Sasquatch came up to Jack to inform him all repairs were completed, and Gret had 100% of her systems running. They planned to fly Gret out from under the mountain the next morning after ensuring her cloaking equipment was fully operational. They did not want to risk the governments of the world seeing a giant spacecraft suddenly appear.

They knew the shock to be great enough learning about Gret and the Sasquatch, using diplomatic methods without suddenly seeing it appear in their satellite feeds. From her travels throughout different galaxies and universes, Gret knew not to suddenly appear. It took cautious communication to avoid panic and misunderstanding. The last thing they needed was to have governments suddenly scramble military aircraft out of fear and attack them. Although no military powers on Earth had a weapon that could have any effect on Gret, she knew the importance of not surprising them. Keeping civilians away from the ship was equally important until they could establish proper safety measures. Jack's uncle Mick would use his business channels to communicate with governments around the world, to inform them of their existence and plans for space travel. Once all the world's governments had been contacted and meetings between them completed, they could bring the government diplomats and scientists to meet Gret in person. They would avoid direct contact with Gret until they knew everything was safe, and only then would she uncloak.

The next morning, after Gret's systems were confirmed operational and her cloaking system turned on, she moved out from underneath the mountain for the first time in nine and a half million years. While Gret began moving, Sasquatch around the globe and in space began continuous monitoring using their advanced technology to determine whether her cloaking systems were operational. After Gret's five-mile-long, four-mile-wide ship's body came out from under the mountain and onto the pad, the Sasquatch reported they could not detect her. Gret knew if the Sasquatch could not detect her with their advanced technology, humans would not be able to either. Everyone involved was relieved that Gret was invisible to humans. The pad they built for Gret, outside the mountain, was large enough that hundreds of different crafts could sit next to her while being hidden by her cloaking. Both humans and Sasquatch will be flying their crafts transporting materials or various species to Gret, which will need to be hidden once they land.

The Sasquatch, Drake and Gret had a meeting to decide when to take that first test flight into space. They would need a few more days testing circuits and systems, said the Sasquatch, before they felt ready for a Space Flight. Gret said she would outfit a couple of her helper robots to cloak the mountain and the pad while they were in space. They all agreed that most humans and Sasquatch must stay on Earth for the first Test flight to be safe. The plan was to hover above Earth while they tested out the systems, then do some high-speed runs across our galaxy. They decided that the first flight should only last two days, and they would plan further test flights if needed depending on how the first went.

After two days of tests on the ground, the Sasquatch announced they were ready for the first flight into space. All nonessential personnel left the ship and were transported by the Sasquatch hypersonic craft into the caverns below. Gret was positive all her systems were in safe working order and there was no danger, but she decided she could not take a chance of losing any of her children. Once everyone not going on the flight was safely in the caverns, Gret prepared for the flight. She moved her robots into position so they could cloak the mountain opening and the pad while they were gone. Uncle Mick stayed on Earth and would be in one of his special labs to monitor the flight, to verify humans did not detect Gret leaving. The Sasquatch, as planned, were manning their labs to see if their instruments could detect Gret as well. A few days earlier, the Sasquatch had launched two of their spaceships, which would monitor Gret while she was in space.

The two Sasquatch spaceships had been outfitted with a faster-than-light drive system and were going to fly along with Gret. Once Gret's test flight was completed, the two Sasquatch ships would fly off in search of their species that it left Earth and had not returned. Normally, Gret would stay in space orbiting a planet, but because she had so many species that needed to be brought on board, it was decided she would land back on Earth. During her first takeoff flight, Gret would be escorted by two Sasquatch craft and two human crafts capable of Space Flight. These crafts would be cloaked, and their job was to monitor Gret as she ascended into space. Once she was in space doing the first set of high-speed tests, the human ships would return to their bases on Earth, and as planned, the Sasquatch ships would accompany Gret. Once her final ground system checks were completed, the Sasquatch and human observation bases gave a go ahead, and the Sasquatch ships in space concurred, and Gret launched.

The moment Gret left the ground, Drake could feel her excitement. She told him, "You are right, my child, I am elated at being able to fly again. I was designed to explore, and being buried was excruciating for me. You will understand the exhilaration of exploration once we are traveling the universe."

Drake was in the flight Control Center with Jack, Michelle, Bear, the pilot, and six Sasquatch when Gret took her first flight in nine and a half million years. Everyone onboard was silently watching the large viewscreen as Gret took off. As if on cue, when Gret finally reached outer space and stopped next to the two Sasquatch space-ships, everyone yelled out. Even Gret herself was yelling. Drake could hear her excitement when she said how wonderful it felt to be in space again. Gret told Drake if she could cry, she would be crying tears of happiness right now. Drake told everyone in the flight control center what Gret had just told him.

Afterward, everyone stood silently for a few moments, then began giving thanks to each other for a great job. The four craft that followed them up into space circled around Gret to inspect for any possible problems. Once they finished their inspections, they let Drake know everything looked good, and then the human ships returned to their home base on Earth. Gret then began running systems diagnostic tests while the Sasquatch on board ran their own. Once all tests were run and systems were confirmed to be in order, Gret announced they were going to take a tour of the solar system.

As a surprise to her children on board, Gret flew through the solar system, circling all the planets to give everyone their first close-up view of them. Though the Sasquatch had been to space before, they had not been able to travel as fast and so smoothly and were impressed. Gret was traveling faster than any Sasquatch or human spacecraft had ever traveled before, but not even near lightspeed. Once she had completely traveled around the solar system, she told Drake to have everyone be prepared to be impressed.

"Sounds like you are going to show off," said Drake.

"Maybe just a little," replied Gret, and suddenly the solar system was gone. The viewscreen blurred for a second, and then they were in a binary star system. A few seconds later, the two Sasquatch ships appeared on their view screen. The pilots aboard the Sasquatch ships contacted the Sasquatch aboard Gret, and everyone in her flight Control Center could hear their excitement. The Sasquatch ships explained they could not believe they were now near Alpha Centauri, which is four and a half lightyears from Earth and only took two seconds to travel there. They said their plans to find the Sasquatch that went into space could now be realized. After the first faster-than-light trip, Gret and the two Sasquatch ships ran a systems analysis to ensure all three ships were in optimal working order. When the Sasquatch were finished running tests on their ships, they announced it was time for them to leave on their journey.

Each of the Sasquatch ships held fifty crew members and were going to explore independently. Having both ships take different routes meant they would be able to search more efficiently. Each of the ships was equipped with an advanced tachyon communication system, which was capable of communication across hundreds of light years. This system would enable the two ships to contact one another if they found some of their species. Since the earlier Sasquatch ships were not capable of faster than lightspeed, they could have only traveled a maximum of two hundred light years in three and a half million years since they left. At most, it would take one minute for a message to reach the other ship, even at one hundred light years.

There are millions of habitable planets within two hundred light years from Earth. The Sasquatch outfitted their ships with Gret's advanced sensors, so they figured it should only take two months to finish the search using the faster-than-light drive. The sensors they installed can detect faint electronic signals that the older Sasquatch would use. Gret was able to track the Sasquatch for a while when they left and had an idea where some of them went. Knowing where to start, even though there were so many planets, would make their search easier and faster.

Drake asked Gret why she was not using the tachyon communication system to communicate with her home planet. Gret said that this type of communication cannot reach most of the home planets that her children came from or hers because the distance was too far. Gret explained her home planet was over seventy-five billion light years away and expanding faster than the speed of light. These distances are too far for this type of communication to reach. With such a great distance, they would have to travel most of the way before the communication system would reach.

"It will take over one hundred and twenty years to reach my home planet," said Gret. "These great distances we travel when we explore are the reason your species need to live virtually indefinitely. You will be surprised at how fast time will go when you can live forever," she added.

"Most species spend much of their time learning and compiling knowledge. It also is important to exercise and find areas of interest to keep your mind and body happy. Drake, with your thirst for knowledge, journeying the galaxies and spending thousands of years learning, will make you incredibly happy. I need to take five or six additional high-speed runs," said Gret, "Does anyone have a place they would like to visit?"

"I have always wondered what the Large Magellanic Cloud Look like in person," said the pilot.

"Good choice," said Gret, "I have been there, and it is beautiful. It should only take us 20 minutes at top speed, which would be a perfect test of the systems and the engine," she added. "Since you produced a destination, it is time for you to take control."

"I cannot believe we are going to travel one hundred sixty thousand light years in 20 minutes," said the pilot.

"Why does not everybody relax while I show the pilot how to prepare for the trip," said Gret.

After they reached the Large Magellanic Cloud, Gret set the filters on the main viewscreen to show the brilliant colors of the cloud. She explained without using special filters that highlighted the various gases and elements, they would only see white stars and darkness. Except for using telescopes, no living human or Sasquatch had ever seen such a sight. It was like looking into a huge cloud of rainbows with billions of shining stars spanning seven thousand lightyears across.

"This is indeed beautiful," said Gret, "but in our journeys, you will see things even more incredible and awe-inspiring. Now, my children, I need to take longer full-speed runs to check out my systems. The next trips will be approximately twelve hours and quite boring. I suggest you all go to the lunchroom, eat, and prepare yourselves for the next forty-eight hours of travel.

"You will learn how to occupy your time while we journey long distances in the future with hobbies, exercising, or studying. I will be running the tests and piloting myself, freeing all of you to relax and do what you choose. While we travel at high speeds, the screens are unable to show our journey, which is why you will learn to keep yourself occupied. In our future travels throughout the galaxies, we will stop often to see the wonders, even on our way to visit your home worlds." Gret went quiet.

Everyone kept busy over the next two days while Gret flew around the galaxies evaluating her systems. She stopped once to show the crew two suns two hundred times the size of Earth's sun, spinning around each other incredibly fast. While they were spinning, each was shedding material out into space, but their gravity pulled the material back into the suns. It looked like two gigantic spinning pinwheels with fire and sparks. Another time, she stopped to show them a planet ten times Earth's size, made up of pure diamonds. She said if they had time, and it would not bankrupt the Earth, they would stop at one of the planets made of gold and bring it home. The crew was in the lunchroom when Gret announced they had reached Earth. Although it had only been two days, everyone was glad to be home. They admitted she was right, space travel is boring, and agreed hobbies and studying were going to be important pastimes in future space travels. Gret then announced she was going to land back on the pad. The landing was so smooth no one knew they were on the ground until Gret told them it was safe to disembark if they wished.

They had only been gone two days, but in that short period of time, they had seen incredible wonders and traveled hundreds of million light years. The flight was successful and Gret's repaired systems performed flawlessly. Gret told Drake she needed to send data to the Sasquatch and human labs so they could analyze what they had seen on the trip. The Sasquatch had traveled into deep space but not as far from Earth as Gret had in just two days. Humans have never been to deep space, so both labs would have data on star systems and planets they could analyze for years. Once they landed, Gret ensured the cloaking system was fully operable, covering the mountain and pad. The Sasquatch and humans contacted their labs to let them know everyone could come back on board. Within hours, dozens of Sasquatch and human crafts were parked under Gret's cloaking sphere. It was not long before hundreds of humans and Sasquatch were back inside the ship, and everything was buzzing with excitement. Drake met with the leaders of the Sasquatch and humans to outline Gret's plans for the near future. The ship was only gone for two days, but it seemed the humans and the Sasquatch had been quite busy while they were gone.

The Sasquatch told Drake they had begun producing small wearable translators from Gret's blueprints. After nine and a half million years, the ones she had on board were long ago useless. Twenty percent of tools and internal components are needed by the voyagers.

"Inside Gret, we are going to have to be rebuilt and replaced after sitting so long and being damaged from the crash. Gret had spent the time repairing only herself because she had not needed those components until now." Drake was informed. It would be up to the voyagers to repair and replace the components they needed. The Sasquatch let Drake know they were not swimmers and would not be any help in contacting the underwater species face-to-face in the water. They could pilot their underwater crafts to take them where they needed to go. With that comment, Mike started to laugh.

"I, for one, can concur the Sasquatch do not know how to swim and do not want to learn," added Mike. The Sasquatch looked at Mike and smiled, all remembering the time he jumped off the cliff into a river to save one of their own and received the nickname Goat for his daring.

"With the translators, there is no need for anyone to get wet," said the Sasquatch, "We were just letting you know do not count on us to go swimming."

"Gret just informed me she would be grateful if we went out to contact the porpoise and dolphins as soon as possible so they could begin training on the ship," said Drake. "As it turns out, the first ones, she wants us to contact work in a US Navy laboratory and an aquatic park in Florida. She believes these are the most advanced intellectually on the planet and will be able to communicate with and quickly train others who are swimming in the wild.

"She told me that one of Uncle Mick's companies is poised to buy an aquatic park in Florida, so talking to the dolphins and porpoises there will not be a problem. Gret believes the US Navy will be more than willing to trade trained dolphins and porpoises for translators and blueprints so that they can build their own. When the Navy finds out the translators can not only translate porpoises and dolphins but every other sentient species on Earth, they will be quite excited to trade. Translators will reduce the training time from years to days for the animals they use in their underwater tactics.

"She wants us to connect with beluga whales also. Research on the Internet will show the handful that have established themselves as being one of the most intelligent of their species. There are wild ones who have interacted with humans, have demonstrated their desire to be with humans, and have shown the highest intelligence. Once you have contacted the first of each species, they will contact others of their species that would also like to journey with us." Drake explained.

"My family is soon to be together," said Gret.

"Gret has spoken," said Drake, "time to get out and find our newest traveling mates. The Sasquatch Hypersonic ships will be best for gathering the species from the oceans, although they say they are not going swimming," He smiled.

"The no swimming part is in the affirmative," said the Sasquatch, smiling back.

"For now, we will be going to zoos around the world to find the smartest of the octopus. It will be much easier than trying to communicate with them underwater. One important warning to everyone," said Gret, "octopi are the biggest jokers and pranksters of all the species we will have onboard. They are not destructive but can be disruptive. During meetings, I have had to shut off their translators to stop them from interrupting and bringing meetings to a standstill. Even with their never-ending humor, the octopi make the best mental health counselors."

There were species Gret brought to Earth nine and a half million years ago that had not evolved enough to join the others on the journey. It would take time before they were sentient enough to understand their history and be able to decide the direction of their future. For now, Gret wanted to journey toward her home world to learn what had transpired while she had been buried for nine and a half million years. On the first trip, she would take only the most advanced species. From the aquatic realm of mammals, dolphins, porpoises, and beluga whales were at the top of the list of species she would be taking. There were a couple of species of octopi that she knew were sentient enough for her to ask if they wanted to go. Killer whales and the larger whales would need more time to evolve and further education before they would be advanced enough to travel in space. In the great ape families, currently, the bonobos, chimpanzees, orangutans and gorillas were sufficiently sentient to understand their history with Gret and the other species to take the journey. Gret was glad to include the avian species in the journey. Macaws, African grey, Crows, and Cockatoos would be the first to join. These birds demonstrated great intelligence and enjoyed human interaction. Gret especially enjoyed watching birds fly inside her on long trips.

Of the primate family, CiCi, the Orangutan from the Leakey research center in Central Borneo, is one of the standouts. She was the leader of the female group. CiCi was also the most intelligent and the precocious of the orangutans. On more than one occasion, she untied a canoe and rowed it down the river, only to bring it back later and tie it back up. It was common to have her come help with chores around camp. One of CiCi's favorite things to do was to help wash laundry. She would work side by side with the woman at the river washing the clothes. She particularly liked the bubbles from the soap. CiCi would laugh and handfuls of them around while she was doing laundry. She taught the other orangutans how to do laundry and how to make and use tools. It was common for her to use sticks or leaves as tools. She even used leaves like gloves to protect her hands when picking prickly fruit.

Everyone in the Research Center swore if CiCi could talk, she would be able to have a conversation with them, she was so smart. Bonobo apes, a close relative to chimpanzees, are the second most advanced of the great apes. They had evolved quickly since they had been living close to humans in protective sanctuaries. Like CiCi, the orangutan and the Bonobos demonstrated high intelligence and a willingness to collaborate with humans. The smartest had shown a great capacity to copy humans and enjoy helping with chores. Their social structure and gentle nature would make a wonderful addition to the family as Gret travels. As with other great apes, the Bonobos had a wonderful sense of humor and were a constant reminder of the importance of having fun. Gret said that once the primate species have a translator of their own, they will lose much of their aggressiveness. They get frustrated from being unable to communicate their feelings, needs and wants. It will be necessary for the next two to three generations to separate aggressive primates from other species until they have reached a higher mental evolution. Those with greater gentleness and higher intellect will be allowed greater access to the other species.

Humans were happy to learn dogs can be brought on board immediately. Being one of the smartest animals on Earth and man's best friend, they were an obvious choice. Once dogs had translators, along with three or four generations to learn and evolve, they would become the best physician's assistants Gret shared with the group.

"Dogs' natural sense of smell gives them a great advantage over even the most advanced machines in diagnosing physical ailments," she added. "Dogs and humans came from the same planet and have always shared a close bond. They were the two most dominant species in their home world, sharing the world in perfect harmony." In sadness, she watched the two species live apart for millions of years until the turmoil on Earth settled enough for the species to reunite. Gret added that they would be the first of the species to begin to have a psychic connection and be able to communicate mentally.

Of all her children, the avian species she felt were the luckiest. Being unable to physically move herself, Gret admired the avian species' ability to fly. If she had a chance to become mortal, she always stated she would want to be a bird. No matter how often she flew around the universes or in space, it always gave her a sense of freedom. The best part about her ability to mentally connect with her children was being in the mind of an avian while they were flying. Their computer quick mind and reflexes made her feel at home. The exhilaration they felt flying made her feel free of the confines she was subject to as a computer.

8

DOLPHINS, PORPOISES AND OTHER SPECIES ARE BROUGHT ON BOARD

T he Sasquatch announced three of their Hypersonic cargo ships capable of carrying the aquatic species were now outside and ready to travel. These ships were larger than they are normal hypersonic craft and had been outfitted with large waterproof tanks. Each ship was given a separate task and group of aquatic species to pick up. Uncle Mick's companies had successfully bought the aquariums and water parks that have the individuals we are searching for, which would enable them to bring in the animals that live there.

The Sasquatch ships would have to stay hidden underwater while the aquatic species were loaded into aquatic containers and transported to them by regular boats. The Sasquatch had given translators to Mick's lab technicians. They have already been in aquariums and water parks, communicating with the chosen aquatic species. Gret let everyone know the aquatic species were excited and looking forward to meeting all the species they would be traveling with. The dolphins have told them their cultural folklore speaks of traveling the stars. The information they were given has already been transmitted around the world to the rest of their species. They can communicate over great distances underwater, and it only took two days for the information to circle the globe. Gret reported dolphins in every location have expressed a desire to join the journey.

One of the Sasquatch cargo ships would be traveling around the world, contacting the wild aquatic species that have demonstrated extremely high intelligence and desire to be around humans. There were examples of individuals from various species throughout the world. There were dolphins and porpoises that have protected humans from sharks or saved them after a shipwreck. As the ship travels around the world, it would be broadcast using a translator calling for volunteers who are interested in traveling with Gret. Once the aquatic species can fully communicate with Gret, sasquatch and humans could begin the process of training them for their various jobs.

9

INFORMING THE GOVERNMENTS AND PEOPLE OF EARTH

U ncle Mick, the Sasquatch, and Gret produced a plan to notify all the world governments of Gret's existence. While they were letting the world know about Gret, they would also inform them of the Sasquatch and the other sentient species that would be traveling with Gret. The group decided it would be best for Uncle Mick to speak at the United Nations and simultaneously broadcast his speech to humans around the world on the Internet, every TV and radio station. The plan was to have Uncle Mick explain who he was, how old he was, and that he owned more companies and was richer than any other human on Earth. He would let them know he was the one who owned the company and oversaw the machinery that had given fresh, clean water to the world. Everyone knew about the water system that was given freely around the world. The fresh water had saved millions of lives worldwide and increased food production, which ended starvation globally. The news about Gret, Sasquatch and the other sentient species would be difficult for most humans to comprehend. Learning that humans and other species came to Earth nine and a half million years ago would be a great shock for everyone. Drake and a Sasquatch would also be with Uncle Mick and speak. Once the meeting was set up at the United Nations in Manhattan, the Sasquatch and human labs began setting up the worldwide broadcast. The next day, Uncle Mick, Drake and the Sasquatch flew to Manhattan.

Gret suggested Mick fly in a Sasquatch fully cloaked craft to have the most psychological impact. She knew from experience the best way to get their attention would be by using advanced technological equipment. It would be able to fly in completely undetected land and be protected from any sort of attack with a force field. Once it landed, they would inform the United Nations leaders and the United States military of its presence. To avoid any military mishaps, they would also inform everyone that no outside aircraft, military equipment, or missiles would be able to approach within ten miles of Manhattan Island until the craft had left. Any aircraft or missile that tried to approach would have its systems shut down and be gently brought to the ground. All other military equipment they tried to use to attack would be disabled and become useless. The park outside the UN building was just the right size for the three-hundred-foot-long glossy black craft to land.

Gret instructed the Sasquatch to not only use the radar cloaking but keep the craft invisible until after it lands for the full psychological effect. The UN was informed to keep the park clear of humans until after the craft landed. Uncle Mick, Drake and one Sasquatch would be the only ones to get out of the craft after it landed. Each would have a translator and a personal force field. The translator was so they could understand everyone who spoke. The force fields were for protection from close contact attacks. The Sasquatch would also wear a cloaking device that made it look like a human so its appearance would not cause a panic. Once the UN members were briefed about what was happening and how the Sasquatch really looked, it would turn it off so they could see its real form.

The flight to Manhattan Island and the UN building went by quickly. Mick, Drake, and the Sasquatch that would be speaking at the UN went over their plans on the way. The pilot interrupted their discussion to inform them they were hovering above the grassy park outside the UN and were ready to land. The pilot added there were people standing outside the building, but the grassy area was clear for landing.

The Sasquatch craft was completely silent and no one on the ground below realized it was hovering above. After the craft landed, the pilot disengaged the cloaking device, and everyone inside watched with amusement at the reaction of the people on the ground. Virtually everyone standing around when the craft uncloaked was startled and jumped. Even though they could not hear, they could tell some of the spectators screamed, some ran away, most jumped back and looked scared. It was obvious most of the people outside were ambassadors, but they could see a few security personnel. A quick scan by the instruments identified weapons that the security personnel were carrying. One of the preconditions of Mick and the others visiting was that there were to be no weapons present. Once all the weapons were identified, the Sasquatch rendered them useless without harming the individuals carrying them. It was a simple matter to change the ammo's chemical composition, which made it incapable of igniting. The chemical change inside each of the cartridges would not be noticed by any of the individuals carrying weapons. As far as they knew, their weapons were still functional, so they would feel safe and not cause a distraction.

Once all the weapons were neutralized, Uncle Mick, Drake, and the Sasquatch disembarked the craft. When the crowd saw them leave the craft, they appeared to relax and started walking towards it. Gret informed Drake that they should stand near the craft and let the crowd come to them. She felt they would relax more if they could look at the incredible craft that was unlike anything they had ever seen. Mick, Drake, and the Sasquatch had communication devices so they could talk with the technicians inside the craft. One of the technicians informed them that the first few individuals approaching were obviously security because of the weapons they were carrying. Even if their weapons had been in working order, the individual protective forcefield each wore would have kept them safe.

The security personnel got close but kept twenty feet of distance from the three that had just got off the craft. Uncle Mick recognized the first ambassador who stepped up to greet them. He had met him before during a few business meetings and greeted him cordially. He was the secretary general of the United Nations and, for all intents and purposes, the head boss of the UN. As the ambassadors came forward one by one, they introduced themselves, and Mick, in turn, introduced Drake and the human-looking cloaked Sasquatch. It was obvious most of the ambassadors were more interested in the incredible craft than they were in the three new visitors. The craft was three hundred feet long and shiny, glossy black, nothing like they had ever seen in their lives. After greeting many of the ambassadors and watching them stare in awe at the craft, Mick suggested they go inside the UN and begin their meeting.

Once all the ambassadors were seated, Uncle Mick stepped up to the podium. Mick introduced himself and explained who he was. He told them what about all the businesses that he owned, that he was the one that built the water system for the world. When he told them his true age, they all started talking excitedly. He had to ask them to please settle down and that he would answer their questions soon. Mick told them that his true age was the least of the amazing things they were going to hear that day. Mick informed everyone that everything that was talked about inside the UN today would be simultaneously broadcast over every radio, TV, telephone, and computer around the world, for every human to hear. He introduced Drake and explained Drake Would be telling them about the true history of humans, so please be as quiet and patient as possible. He added that much of what Drake was going to disclose would be hard to believe and comprehend but was the absolute truth. Any questions they had would have to wait until after Drake finished speaking. Mick stepped aside, and Drake stepped up to the podium to speak.

Drake introduced himself and explained where he was born and about his early life. He talked about being able to hear a voice in his head for as long as he can remember. When he got to the part about finding a cave in the mountains with something in it, the room went completely silent with the expectation. Drake explained that the voice in his head asked him to walk into the cave but remain calm about what he was going to see. When he described the giant crystal spaceship inside, the ambassadors all started talking at once. It took a couple minutes for Drake to get them to calm down to finish listening to what he had to say.

Drake went on to tell them that the voice in his head that he had been hearing his whole life was coming from the spaceship. Then he explained the spaceship itself was a sentient computer named Gret. When he told them the spaceship crashed nine and a half million years ago, Drake could tell they were shocked, but that shock was nothing compared to their reaction when he told them that humans were on that spaceship when it crashed. It took 10 minutes before Drake could quiet them down enough to continue talking. Once everyone had quieted down, he explained that Gret was going to be speaking to them next.

The huge monitor on the wall behind Drake turned on, and a crystal spaceship appeared. It was apparent the spaceship was extremely large, and as the view panned around the outside of the ship, a voice started to speak. To all the ambassador's surprise, the voice was female and simultaneously spoke to each person in their own language. She introduced herself as Gret and explained she was going to tell them the history of humans and some of the species on Earth. As Gret talked, the view on the monitor showed the complete exterior of the spaceship, then began showing the inside. She explained how a cosmic accident had buried her, killed the species that were aboard her, and that only some of the species that had been exploring on Earth had survived. She told how, over millions of years after the crash, the surviving species de-evolved and some re-evolved.

Gret told them some species, after evolving sufficiently, left Earth and never returned, but some had returned and stayed. When Gret told the ambassadors she wanted one of the species that came to Earth with her nine and a half million years ago to speak to them today, the place began to buzz with excitement. She let them know that this species had re-evolved faster than humans and had gone to space over three million years ago. She added that they watched as humans became more advanced but chose to hide for their own protection as human technology advanced enough they were a minor threat to this species. Gret told how this species had sent spaceships everywhere to discover their true origins because they were not able to communicate with Gret. She let them know that this species she was going to introduce, and many of the species, including humans, would soon be leaving Earth to visit their original home worlds. The last statement caused major excitement amongst the ambassadors. Gret let them speak to one another for a few minutes before asking them to calm down and listen again. She explained which species would be going and how the humans that would be going were picked. She assured them there would be humans from every country on Earth along, so no one country would need to feel left out. Gret asked for calm and quiet because it was now time for them to meet the species that had been watching humans and been to space over three million years ago. The Sasquatch, which was cloaked to look human, stepped up to the mic. Many ambassadors asked if this was a different species and why it looked human. Gret explained that she did not want them to be scared by its natural appearance, so it was disguised to look human. She asked all of them to relax and not be afraid of this species because it was harmless. Before un-cloaking, the Sasquatch spoke to the ambassadors.

"I want to thank all of you, gentle humans, for coming today it began. My species has been watching and taking care of humans for many thousands of years. Until the last few hundred years, we worked side by side with many of your cultures. Once you became technologically advanced enough to possibly harm our people, we hid from you but never quit working with some of your cultures. As Gret stated, my species has been to space and explored the cosmos. Millions of years ago, we sent many spaceships out to explore in hopes of finding our true origins. It was not until meeting Gret that we learned the truth.

"At this moment, we have new, faster ships, thanks to Gret, in search of those ships so we may learn their fate. My species has been working with and protecting your people for millions of years. There are dangers our two species face from outer space, which we have worked to protect Earth from. With Gret's much more advanced technology, it will be easier to carry out the task of protecting Earth and its inhabitants. It was my species that gave Mick the technology for the water system that he installed around the globe a few years ago. We have many other projects that will be implemented to abolish issues like famine, disease, and even dangerous medical conditions once our two species have fully met and come to an agreement. We will be introducing many scientific advancements that will make your species healthier and even live longer.

"There is a coming cosmic danger that will require our two species, and a few other species, that you will be introduced to later, to live in the underground caverns we have built around the globe. We will be talking about that in the future, but now is the time for me to uncloak so that you may see my true appearance. Before I uncloak, you all must relax and be prepared for my real appearance. As Gret explained before, I am not human, and I am in no way dangerous."

The Sasquatch stepped away from the podium and un-cloaked. The room was suddenly filled with gasps and shuffling of uncomfortable bodies. Gret spoke to each of the ambassadors, calming them and reminding them they were in no danger. Once the room had settled, the Sasquatch stepped back behind the podium to speak.

"Many of you have heard stories or seen pictures of my species, and now you can see we do indeed exist. Once my species returned from exploring space, we decided to live in balance with nature. Through many generations, our bodies changed and things like clothes were not needed. We planted the Earth around our settlements, so they were self-supporting. For protection, we built caves and huge caverns that required no power source and were self-supporting. We have remained in balance for over three million years. It is now time for us to work with the human species to accomplish the same balance for you. The water system Mick's company built was just the beginning.

"Over the next few years, we will build gardens around your towns and cities that will completely feed the populations. Our power sources are environmentally clean and will be installed so you have the power you need but at no cost to the environment. In a few years, we will transition into the underground caverns for both our species. Once the dangerous energy from space that will bathe Earth is here, it will be dangerous for our species to dwell on the surface. There are still many years to prepare and get accustomed to each other. My species will share our knowledge and science with humans so you may feel confident and secure."

When the Sasquatch finished talking, Gret announced it was time for them to leave. They had much to do to prepare for the future, and she knew the UN ambassadors would like to talk amongst themselves.

Drake, Mick, and the Sasquatch said their goodbyes and walked to the ship. There was a crowd by the ship, but once they saw the Sasquatch, they moved away quickly. Everyone talked on the way back to the mountain where Gret was. They agreed the meeting was a success. The Sasquatch smiled deeply when Drake commented on the reaction of the humans when he un-cloaked and as it walked to the ship.

"My species is used to human's reactions to us," it commented. "In times past when we worked closely with humans, they weren't so scared."

"I can say that I, too, was a bit scared," said Drake.

"The first time I saw one of your species, my reaction was indeed fear," said Mick. Once they landed at the mountain, they all began getting ready for the next phase of getting the human population and governments ready for integration into Gret's influence. Mick and the Sasquatch began planning with Gret how to best naturalize the human weapons without causing panic.

10

BRINGING THE WORLD
COMMUNITIES INTO ONE FAMILY

The first step in uniting all countries was for Gret to make weapons of mass destruction unable to function. Without bombs or missiles, deadly chemicals, warplanes, warships, tanks, and artillery of any kind, no army around the world could be the aggressor. They would effectively demilitarize the whole world. If no country could attack another, all wars would cease, and global peace could be achieved. It was decided that as soon as all weapons were nullified, Gret would simultaneously broadcast what they had accomplished to every government and human. They would also inform the citizens of the world at the same time. They would inform the governments and the citizens the world was now safe from war. Once all the governments and the world population knew they were safe from war, they could begin to live in peace as a species. The decision was made so that the people of Earth could choose what caverns they wanted to occupy. There were enough caverns that only 20,000 individuals needed to occupy a single cavern, and they still had caverns left over. This meant there would never be overcrowding or a need to worry about resources. Allowing each species and individual adequate space would avoid the chance of confrontation due to stress. The Sasquatch knew some cultures and species liked to be in larger groups, so they would allow some to form larger societal centers but would limit total numbers in a single cavern. All nations would be able to design their layouts.

The Sasquatch knew that once everyone had plenty of space and the resources they needed to survive, peace would be easier to maintain. Everyone would have free range of all the caverns and highly advanced technology. They also knew that once all the cultures and species had settled in and learned how to communicate, the time in the caverns would be enjoyable for all. The biggest surprise would be how long they would be able to live inside the caverns. From experience, the Sasquatch knew that being able to live long lives would greatly impact the attitude of all the species inside the caverns. When all humans felt safe, incidences of conflict would lessen. It was almost always hunger and lack of adequate space that caused wars. With so many caverns around the world, space was not an issue. It was time for Gret to announce to the world governments and all the people that all weapons of mass destruction would be made inoperable. The Sasquatch, Drake, Uncle Mick, and the Sasquatch prepared for the broadcast to all governments and humans about the disbarment. It was decided that Gret would make the announcement so there would be no animosity towards any human or Sasquatch. Gret sent messages to each government, radio, TV, computer, phone, and electric sign that there was going to be an important world broadcast in a few hours. When it was time, Gret began talking.

Gret began by introducing herself and explaining her history and the human journey with her. She told the complete story, even about the Sasquatch and other sentient species on Earth. She told them that all humans deserved to be safe and able to live without fear. Gret explained there were governments and individuals that meant to harm others and needed to be stopped. As she was talking, unknown to the governments, all weapons of mass destruction, down to the smallest bomb and hand grenade, were made non-functional. It was decided that even handguns and rifles would not be allowed anymore. There would be plenty of food, so no one needed a gun to hunt.

Gret told the humans that large-scale aggression needed to stop and the only way to accomplish it was complete disarmament across the globe. She let them know there would be personal forcefield devices available for each human. These were wearable devices that would protect them from humans that meant them harm and animals that were dangerous. She explained that now there were no bombs or weapons left on Earth that could do harm. She told them that humans were not given a choice in this disarmament, but it was not a choice they would have ever made, so it was necessary for the safety of all sentient beings on Earth. Now, every country and human was equally safe.

While Gret was talking, every government and human began checking their weapons. Within minutes, ambassadors from around the world were contacting one another, checking to see if they each had lost all weapons. Gret announced that at that moment, all weapons had been neutralized, even individuals' guns of all types. She informed them that from that moment on, even if someone tried to make a gun, it would not work. It was the right of all beings to be safe from harm and aggression. She informed the humans there were now stockpiles of personal forcefield devices around every village, town, and city immediately available for use if wanted. These force-fields would even protect them from most falls and drowning. No knife or animal claw could hurt them while they had it turned on.

Gret then apologized for not allowing governments and individuals the opportunity to make their own decisions on the matter of disarmament but stated that humans never would have been able to agree to disarm. For the safety of humanity and other sentient beings on Earth, it was necessary for her to do it. The governments of Earth were in a panic, trying to decide what to do and were in contact with each other trying to determine if any government still had operatable weapons. Within a few hours, the panic in the governments subsided once it was determined that no country had weapons.

The most amazing thing to Gret was how people from all over the globe took to the streets to celebrate. Once they knew they were free from the oppression from their own governments and no country could attack, they filled the streets. Gret began broadcasting the celebrations from around the globe to all governments and individuals to show the world how elated everyone was to be free from fear. This was the beginning of world peace, and all humans could feel the change. Before she signed off, Gret told the world that this was just the beginning of safety, happiness, and prosperity for all species.

11

IT WAS TIME TO BRING THE REST OF
THE CREW ON BOARD

G ret announced to Drake her systems were functioning one hundred percent and all the species' habitats were operational. It was time to begin loading the sentient species that were going to travel with her back into space. The Sasquatch had been contacting the various sentient species that would travel. Now was time to head out and collect them for the journey. The hardest to pick up and transport were the aquatic species. The Sasquatch ships had been modified and were ready to begin. All that was left to do was inform all the species that had been contacted to prepare for pickup. Once all the crafts left to pick up the various species, the Sasquatch and humans onboard Gret began preparing for the arrival of their new traveling partners. It would only be a few hours for the first crafts to arrive back to Gret, so the humans and Sasquatch put on their universal translators and took their positions. Every new species had its own space inside Gret. The aquatic species would share the water-filled quarters. There were three aquatic areas for them to live in and one where they could work and interact with other species. Many of the non-aquatic species would use underwater breathing equipment and translators so they could enjoy close time with the aquatic species.

It was important that the great ape species have their own separate sections until they had evolved further so that they were not as aggressive. Being able to easily communicate with other species would help eliminate some frustration and aggression, but Gret said the different species need a bit more protection from the great apes for now. The dogs were going to be fine living with humans and Sasquatch, especially with translators helping them communicate easily.

When the first craft arrived, it docked onto the outside of the ship and began loading. Everyone onboard Gret was excited to watch their new brothers and sisters come on board. The first craft was a group of the great apes. They all had their translators on and could communicate once on the ship to anyone. It would be important to keep each ape species separate until they were not aggressive to each other. The gorillas were the biggest worry and had a large, separate environment. The bonobos, chimpanzees and orangutans were, for the most part, harmless but still needed a separate environment in the beginning. Many of them would have a free run of the ship and be able to integrate with humans and Sasquatch most of the time.

Dogs were on the second craft that arrived. That craft was landed outside the main entry and the dogs came running into the ship like a crazy group of happy kids. With translators, it was the first time humans and dogs could speak to each other in over nine million years. The dogs had much to say after so long. As always, the dogs were excited to see the humans and quickly began talking and playing. The children were the most excited among the humans about the dogs and began playing with the dogs immediately, much to the pleasure of the dogs. Everyone was laughing as the kids played. The dogs were extremely curious about the Sasquatch as well. Dogs have always been able to smell and find the Sasquatch, but now they could talk and understand them.

When the first craft with birds arrived, it docked inside Gret so there would not be too much confusion until they had their translators. Once the birds had been fitted with their translators, they had free run of Gret. Birds were a favorite of Grets. She enjoyed their freedom and ability to fly like she could. Once the birds were flying around, the rest of the species stood in awe as the birds flew around the ship with incredible glee. Their aerobatics entranced all who stared in wonder at their ability to fly with speed and grace without hitting anything.

The last crafts were the ones with the aquatic species. More crafts were needed because of the need for water to transport them. The crafts docked onto the outside of Gret for unloading. Once inside Gret, the aquatic species began talking to everyone. The octopi instantly began planning their jokes. Gret had told them of their exploits onboard before the crash, and they wanted to begin where they had left off over nine million years ago. Gret knew she might regret bringing the octopi back onboard but enjoyed their humor so much it was worth it. The dolphins and other aquatic species came onboard and were in wonder at all the technology. Once they slowed down a bit, they began communicating with all the other species. The aquatic species asked the others to visit often in their water world. Even the birds were happy to talk about visiting. Birds and aquatic species have always gotten along, and now that they could communicate, it would be more enjoyable.

As the various species got to know one another, Gret told Drake how wonderful it felt to have her children home again. Her dream of traveling the stars again was almost upon them.

"It will not be long before we are in space again, so it is time we prepare the world and all my children for the journey," said Gret. Drake agreed and went to the control room, where he sent out a communication to all those responsible for preparing Gret for space flight. As soon as he made the announcement, the feeling in the ship became electric. It was as though Drake could read the minds of hundreds of his fellow space travelers. Gret instantly told him that was what it was, and she could hear many more herself.

12

LEAVING FOR THE MOTHER WORLD

G ret told Drake she had wondered for nine and a half million years what happened to her home planet.

"I was constructed on a different planet than you were born on," said Gret. "We will stop at all the planets where each of your species came from on our way to my home planet. Many species, throughout time, have wondered where they came from. We will not have very many different species on this journey, so it will not take exceptionally long to stop at each planet. It will take over one hundred years to reach my planet. Best to get everyone fully engaged in ways to keep busy during transit between stops. With long lifespans, it makes it easier to travel the great distances of space, but without ways to keep occupied, the travels would become deadly boring." Gret had been preparing all the species for various activities, training, and learning, encouraging them to practice before taking off. Many of the species wanted mostly to become more familiar with other species. They had their own keep busy ideas, but speaking with a different species was at the top of the list for many.

Drake knew having so many different species would make things more interesting. Some of the species, like the octopi, will keep everyone on their toes with their constant jokes.

"One time," said Gret, "the octopus shut off the artificial gravity, and even the aquatic species had a bit of trouble. I learned from my mistakes how to keep those jokers in check, at least I am hoping. The dogs had been the most fun to observe." Drake could hear the happiness in her voice. "They were always friendly before the crash, but now they seemed even more so. The dogs have even been playing in the aquatic environment. The dolphins and dogs get along better now than nine million years ago. My children are a funny bunch and travels shall be interesting. The sasquatch and human kids cannot seem to get enough of each other, and the dogs are constantly playing with them as well. This will be a most enjoyable journey."

Once everything was ready for takeoff, Gret announced their departure to the world. She assured them she would keep in constant contact and that the Sasquatch ships would soon be arriving from their mission to reconnect with their own travelers. Gret let all the governments know they would soon be outfitted with spaceships like the Sasquatch ones so they may also explore. No one would be left out of the technology loop. Uncle Mick's companies and the Sasquatch would make sure everyone had a long and prosperous life. Within a few years, humans would need to begin moving into the caverns, but anyone or any country that wanted could begin moving in immediately.

Gret had Drake pilot the ship into orbit. Once in space, she said goodbye to all the humans on Earth. Gret announced to all her travelers that they would be stopping at their original home worlds along the way to her own. Anyone who wanted to stay in their old home world would be allowed if it were safe and if the inhabitants would allow it.

"In one hundred years, I will be home," Gret said to Drake with a slight sigh, and in a flash of light, they were gone.

ABOUT THE AUTHOR

Patrick Talmadge Sr. has always been a late bloomer. His growth didn't cease until he was over 21 years old. He reached his pinnacle as a national and world-class masters middle-distance runner at the age of 37, when he won his first master's national track and field championship in the 800-meter run.

At 47, Patrick earned his Bachelor of Arts degree and made history as the oldest NCAA cross-country runner. Seven years later, at 54, he returned to college to pursue a Master's degree in Psychology. During this time, he ran the mile in track, once again setting a record as the oldest NCAA track and field runner. He received his Master's degree in Psychology at 57. At the age of 66, he embarked on his writing journey.

Patrick taught himself to read at the tender age of three and a half and has been an avid reader ever since. With a keen interest in all fields of science, science fiction, and fantasy, he amassed a wealth of knowledge that would later prove invaluable when he began writing. Throughout his 20s and 30s, Patrick devoured two to three books a day. Upon graduating from graduate school in 2011, he retired from competitive running and felt a growing desire to write the stories that had been simmering within him.

In November 2021, spurred on by the love of his life, Patrick began his writing career. By July 2023, he had completed an adult four-book science fiction series about Sasquatch, a four-book children's series on the same subject, and a standalone novel about a senior community that befriends a troupe of Sasquatch.

Patrick possesses a unique ability to write multiple stories simultaneously, allowing him to modify and adjust interconnected narratives for clarity when writing a series. With a bit of luck, Patrick will continue to pursue his passion for writing for the rest of his life, or at least until his computer gives out.

ALSO BY PATRICK TALMADGE

Hidden Mountain Chronicles

Sasquatch Race

Sasquatch Prison Diary

Tenino Caverns

Sasquatch Home Planet

Sasquatch Chronicles

Hunter and Noah vs. Sasquatch Vol. 1

Hunter and Noah vs. Sasquatch Vol. 2

Hunter and Noah vs. Sasquatch Vol. 3

Hunter and Noah vs. Sasquatch Vol. 4

Sasquatch Senior Community Series

Sasquatch Senior Community

Sasquatch Senior Community: Lois and Mel the Beginning

Sasquatch Senior Community: The Early Years

Sasquatch Senior Community: The Middle Years

AFTERWORD

Go to hangaripublishing.com to learn more about the Authors and stay up to date with their newest releases.

www.ingramcontent.com/pod-product-compliance
Lightning Source LLC
Chambersburg PA
CBHW071208120626
46546CB00006B/2465